---------- ★ ----------

FOR SUCH A CAREFUL HOUSEKEEPER, SHE HAD AN AWFULLY MESSY BEDROOM

Then I realized what the mess w~~~~
tered and splashed ~~~~
sheets.

Rena's bare foo~~~~
clothes. It wasn'~~~~
if it were going t~~~~

I opened the doc~~~~ to force some order into what I was seeing, but the essential wrongness of it kept confusing me. Moments passed while I tried to make the thing sprawled across the bed add up to Rena: foot, leg, arm . . . yes, right there ought to be, *had* to be . . .

I was looking for her face, but her face was gone. What remained of her mouth was full of blood. Masses of stuff stuck to the headboard: hair, and so on, glued there with gore.

I stumbled back.

---------- ★ ----------

Kittredge's "descriptions give one a chill, as does a scary ending."
—The Armchair Detective

"Delightfully entertaining."
—The Virginian Pilot and Ledger Star

A Forthcoming Worldwide Mystery by
MARY KITTREDGE

DEAD AND GONE

Murder in Mendocino

MARY KITTREDGE

WORLDWIDE®

TORONTO · NEW YORK · LONDON · PARIS
AMSTERDAM · STOCKHOLM · HAMBURG
ATHENS · MILAN · TOKYO · SYDNEY

MURDER IN MENDOCINO

A Worldwide Mystery/September 1990

Published by arrangement with Walker and Company.

ISBN 0-373-26055-5

Thanks to all who helped:
Kevin O'Donnell, Jr., Mark J. McGarry,
Richard Curtis, Ruth Cavin,
and especially to
John Ellerson Squibb

This book is for my mother and father,
Elizabeth Agnes Talbot
and
Richard Truman Talbot
and for
Harris Squibb

ONE

MY AGENT, BERNIE HOLLOWAY, started work at nine that day and called me as soon as he got to his desk. His desk, however, is in Manhattan, while mine is in the attic den of my cottage in Mendocino County, three thousand miles and three time zones to his west.

Bernie knows about time zones, but he also knows I have a telephone on my bedside table. Furthermore, he suspects my resistance is lowest when I am asleep.

"Plywood," he suggested when I had fumbled the receiver to my ear. "Charlotte, sweetheart, I've got the contracts right here. *A Hundred and One Perfect Plywood Projects*—"

"No plywood," I said. "No paneling." I pulled the flannel sheets over my head, to keep the dawn out of my eyes. "No more do-it-yourself books, Bernie. Are you getting the picture?"

"That's it! Picture windows! Charlotte, darling, you're a genius. I'll have the contracts expressed right out—"

"Bernie," I said. "Read my lips. N-O. No."

"Ha-ha," he said. "You don't mean this. At least, I hope you don't. The *Home Digest* folks are solid employers, Charlotte, they pay well and they pay *on time*—"

"It's six o'clock in the morning here, Bernie." I burrowed my head deeper into the pillows. "I never lie to you before noon."

Or hardly ever, I added silently. Bernie was not silent, because he is never silent. Bernie regards silent time as wasted time, especially when the call is on his nickel.

"Charlotte. Listen to me. I know you have ambition—"

"Right. My ambition today was to sleep until eight."

"—and I would be the first to tell you that you have a wonderful, wonderful talent..."

Bernie is a fine fellow, but he chases his commissions the way some lawyers chase ambulances. In fact, I think he will chase the occasional ambulance, if he thinks the passenger will come out with one typing finger intact. What Bernie calls "victim books" are very hot this season.

"...*Home Digest* will buy as many of these things as you can crank out, don't you see? You can knock off six of the little suckers every year for the rest of your life. And at five grand a pop, sweetheart, you've got a *gold mine*..."

Six a year.

"...Everyone's got to have a hobby, and the way I see it, why, it's just one hand washing the other..."

Every year.

"...You write the do-it-yourself books, so the customers get their hobbies, and in return they finance your, uh, *creative* writing..."

For the rest of my life.

"...in your *spare* time. Charlotte? Are you there?"

"I'm here. Let me just make sure I've got this straight, Bernie, all right?"

"Of course," he said.

"You told *Home Digest* you've got me in the bag. I know you did, so there's no use denying it. You promised I'd write them six books a year, when I *told* you I'm fed up with home repair, that I want to do something else. Starting now."

"Charlotte," he began, smelling danger at last, "you know I have the greatest respect—"

"But I can't spend respect, can I, Bernie? And more to the point, neither can you."

Bernie cleared his throat the way he always does when he is backpedaling like mad, trying to buy time to get out of one approach and into another.

"Charlotte, I am morally and professionally certain that you can make a marvelous book out of this, uh, *historical* project you have in mind, but until you do, just until you get established—"

"I *am* established. You have made that clear. An established hack is what I am, and what I need now is to get unestablished, fast. Because if I don't do it fast I am never going to, ever. And do you know why, Bernie?"

I paused, but if he did know why, he also knew better than to say so.

"Because I will be too busy writing step-by-step project instructions for someone who, if he had any brains, would go out and hire a professional and get the job done right, that's why!"

"I have only been looking out for your best interests," Bernie said.

"Right. I know you have. Now be a good guy, and let me do the looking out for a while. If I write one more word about how to hang an interior door, I'll hang my*self*."

He sighed. "All right, all right. Just don't say I didn't warn you. It's a jungle out there, Charlotte, I'm selling good stuff for a nickel a word."

"A nickel a word? You mean, to the pulps? Wait a minute—is that before or after your ten percent?"

"Before," he said. "And yes, pulps. The slicks are all backlogged to hell and gone—they won't be buying again until fall. Besides, it's fifteen percent on sales under a thousand, you know that, Charlotte—"

"Fifteen?"

Fifteen percent is not a commission. Fifteen percent is a mugging.

"Oh," he said. "Oh, but you *wouldn't* have known that, would you? No, of course not ... oh, my. Those *horrid Home Digest* books. Spoiled you a bit, dear. Made you a wee tad overconfident—"

"Bernie. Wait a minute, Bernie."

"—as you'll discover. Why, you've never made less than a thousand on anything in your life, have you, Charlotte?"

"Damn it, Bernie, you listen to me—"

"Until *now*, you haven't." Then he hung up.

I lay back in bed, my hand on the telephone, and began to count slowly: one thousand one ... one thousand two ...

Outside, it was raining. Droplets plinked in the gutters. A stain shaped like Africa spread very slowly on the ceiling just over my head. Tar paper, I thought; shingles, nails, aluminum ladder.

... one thousand ten. The telephone rang.

"Charlotte?"

"I'm here, Bernie."

"You know I meant it, don't you? About your best interests, I mean. I care about you, Charlotte, really I do."

"I know." I threw back the blankets and sat up, abandoning all hope of any more sleep. I'd had hopes the night before, too, and the bed was littered with evidence of them: two paperback thrillers, the King James Bible, last Sunday's *Times* crossword and a scattered deck of Bicycle playing cards.

"I just want you to be able to make a decent living in this racket," Bernie said.

"It's not the decent living part that bothers me." I gathered the cards and stacked them all face down in the palm of my right hand. "And I know it's sort of a racket at your end. But when it starts feeling like a racket at *my* end..."

"Okay, okay." Bernie sighed. "You people and your damned artistic temperaments." He made it sound as if artistic temperament ought to be bred out of writers, like crossed eyes out of Siamese cats.

Personally, I like my cats cross-eyed. At that moment, in fact, a set of crossed eyes regarded me with near-sighted impatience from the heap of blankets at the foot of the bed.

"Meerowryeeow," Ninki said, which meant: *If you don't give me my breakfast this minute, I'm going out to dismember a chipmunk*.

Ignoring her, I divided the cards with my thumb, curling my index finger up under the bottom half of the pack. The deck felt greasy, but the top cards slid back toward my other fingers: so far, so good.

"... strictly up-to-date on what you're doing," Bernie said. "Maybe send me a rough draft."

"Uh-huh." Slowly, slowly. The top half of the deck balanced on the upturned edges of the bottom cards.

Bernie knew perfectly well that I wasn't going to follow his advice. No one would see my current project, not a word, until it was finished. I'd gone the show-and-tell route with other books, and it was a mistake. Still, Bernie felt obliged to give me his best shot.

"...just because it's art doesn't mean we can't try to get you a deal on it ..."

"Right," I said, watching the cards.

If I gave him a rough draft, he would have suggestions. He might even show it around to editors, who also would have suggestions, and being no fool, I would probably follow some of the suggestions. Pretty soon I would be wondering who was the writer here, anyway, and soon after that I wouldn't know the answer. It was good business, but it was a hell of a way to write a book. Besides, if I wanted to do business there was always *Home Digest*.

I pushed the cards another fraction. Then, cheating, I steadied the pack with the index finger of my right hand. The cards promptly toppled into my lap, which just went to show you can't do card tricks by committee, either.

"...an outline, at least, and a couple of chapters," Bernie said.

Miffed at being ignored, Ninki leapt to the floor and stalked towards the door, her tail semaphoring *so long, sucker*. Realizing too late that she meant it, I swung my legs hastily out of bed, pulling the telephone along with me.

"...try to get a contract, so at least you wouldn't be working on spec ..."

I made a fast grab, caught my big toe in the phone wire, and tripped on the curled-up edge of the braided rug. Ninki sidestepped gracefully. Then, tossing back one cross-eyed glance of disdain, she vanished around the corner.

"...a right way and a wrong way to do these things," he went on.

In the kitchen, the cat door flapped open and shut.

"Ninki, you come back here this instant!"

"...huh?" Bernie said.

WHEN I MOVED TO NORTHERN CALIFORNIA, the real estate lady said I would be able to hear the foghorns off the coast, two miles from my cottage in the redwoods. Wisely, she neglected to tell me the reason, which is that sound carries well under water, and water is what our atmosphere mostly is, for most of the winter. It was now January fifteenth; I yearned with religious fervor for April and the dry season, when I would skimp on showers and fill my toilet tank with rocks.

Meanwhile, I peered out into the drizzle and called for Ninki. The air was chill, perfumed with sea salt and wet evergreens; great billows of fog moved silently: wandering ghosts among the redwoods. I stepped off the porch onto a spongy mat of pine needles, inches deep.

A bell-buoy clanked; a foghorn honked back froggily: *bow-whonnk*. Stray breezes shivered in the high branches, sending down brief, pattering showers.

No response from Ninki, however; she was probably in the shed, cruising the woodpile in search of fresh meat. Irritated with her, I went back inside and shoved the coffeepot under the faucet and gave the faucet handle a sharp, satisfying twist.

Whereupon the entire faucet assembly came up in my hand. Water gouted up in a fountain, spattering the ceiling, the floor.

Under the sink, the shut-off valve handle twirled uselessly on its rust-frozen stem. Pliers dug bright grooves in the metal but produced no further effect. Shoemakers' kids go barefoot, I thought, remembering the sage advice I had recently written on this very problem. Then a horrid suspicion struck me, and I backed hurriedly out of the cabinet, water trickling down my back in a chilly stream.

It was as I had thought; the pool on the floor was rapidly approaching a metal grate. Under that grate lay my enemy, Furnace. If the water doused Furnace's pilot light, I would have to relight it by wedging a wooden kitchen match into a loop at the end of a straightened-out wire coat-hanger, lowering the lit match down the hole, and pushing two buttons while turning an extremely unreliable knob.

Thinking of this, I grabbed a hammer and gave the valve-stem a solid smack. The valve slammed shut, stripping its threads. The merry fountain faltered and collapsed. The pool stopped a quarter-inch short of Furnace.

I mopped up the water and sat down on the floor, breathing hard. Behind me, the cat door opened and closed. The sink now resembled a carcass deserving only of a hasty burial, as did the smaller, bloodier carcass which Ninki chose at that moment to deliver, apparently in the hope that a little snack might make me feel better.

I chased her back outside, flung the chipmunk after her, closed the cat door, scanned the wreckage of the sink, got dressed, and decided to drive into town for breakfast. Which was how I discovered that, for getting and keeping my attention, there is nothing like a shotgun blast.

THE LOAD OF BUCKSHOT missed the Volkswagen's windshield by inches and tore on into a bay laurel thicket. An instant later came the *ka-whack*. I slammed on the brakes, jumped out of the car, and hit the ground running. That little bastard was going to get it.

The little bastard was Joey Dolan, a twelve-year-old friend of mine from next door. At least he was usually a friend; there were times, like right now, when I thought he ought to be clapped into leg irons. Shoving through the strip of thick brush which formed a sort of demilitarized zone between his place and mine, I emerged into the Dolan compound.

Their porch sagged onto a rusting jack, a rotting stump, and an engine block. A rebel flag hung at one window; the rest were broken and wadded with rags. Alongside the front steps a trash barrel smoldered, thickening the drizzle with greasy smoke. Chicken droppings littered the yard, the steps, the porch, and the floor inside.

The kingpin of this place was Fred Dolan, a tubby, balding little would-be hippie who wore his radical politics the way a slut wears cologne; to cover the stink. The shotgun had been Dolan's birthday gift to his stepson; no instruction, just the weapon. Dolan probably figured the kid would learn shooting naturally, as he'd had to learn everything else.

Unfortunately, Joey's thirst for knowledge extended about to the end of his nose. He liked the sound the big gun made, and that was all.

As I caught sight of him, he was standing on the porch, loading the gun again. I slogged through a vegetable garden run riot: squash vines and lush marijuana plants. It occurred to me that the vegetables on the place were smarter than the people, and I gauged my argument accordingly.

"Joey, I'll bust that gun right over your head!"

Joey was skinny and sallow and sad; he looked as if he lived on Twinkies and Gatorade, which, despite his macrobiotic family, he probably did. What with all the ideological ranting around the joint, nobody had time to watch out for a twelve-year-old's vitamin intake.

"I'll tell Fred," he said. He wore a faded Jefferson Airplane T-shirt, dungarees, Keds. A green sweatband held back some of his dark hair; the rest fell down into his eyes, which he kept blinking as if he were near-sighted. He was shivering.

"You tell Fred he's an intellectual pimp." I clomped up onto the porch, stomping mud off my boots. "You tell him his brains haven't got the powder to blast his own bottom out of this yard. You tell him the range of a twelve-gauge shotgun is sixty-five yards, you sniveling punk, and if I *ever* catch you firing that thing again I'll—"

I stopped. He was crying.

"Jesus, Joey," I said, "where is everyone?"

It struck me that the yard was empty except for some junk cars in which the chickens had taken up roosts. The only sound was the patter of rain, and the chickens' moronic clucking.

Joey shook his head.

"Have you had any breakfast?"

He shook his head again.

"They went to the city." He tried to scrub tears out of his eyes, but succeeded only in spreading dirt around his face.

"Everybody?" Besides his stepfather, Joey's family consisted of his mother, Phyliss, and his seventeen-year-old sister, Liane.

"They had some meeting or something," Joey said. "I don't dig that shit, I just embarrass them. So they left me here."

I took the shotgun from his hands and leaned it against the wall. Beneath the rebel flag it looked like the prop for a rock-and-roll album cover.

"Listen, you want to go down and eat? Down to the Sea Gull?"

He shrugged. "No money."

I thought for a minute about a crew that would leave a kid alone with no money and probably no food except for maybe a few rice cakes and a wad of alfalfa sprouts. Probably some imported coffee to wash it down with, if he could figure out how to grind the beans. And if he were old enough to drink coffee, which he wasn't.

All you need is love, man. I thought if Joey were really a rotten kid, he'd have already learned to use that shotgun.

"Yeah, well, I've got some firewood needs splitting, out in the shed. Hammer and wedge, it'll build your muscles. What do you say, is that worth breakfast?"

He looked at me sideways, shrugging. "I guess. Ain't got nothin' better to do."

"*Haven't* got nothin' better," I admonished him. "Go get a jacket."

TWO

JOEY FIDDLED WITH the car radio, producing only static since we were hemmed in on all sides: to the north and south by ragged coastline, behind us to the east by mountains, and to the west by the sea, which lay straight ahead, beyond the town.

He smelled of wood smoke and old socks. I wanted to wrestle him into a hot soapy shower, and then propel him through a barbershop and a department store. He needed T-shirts, blue jeans, shoes, a new jacket, and probably underwear too.

He needed more than that, in fact. He needed a parent to take care of him. I had to keep reminding myself that I wasn't it. He was twelve, almost thirteen, and still a blank slate, but it was a slate I had no business writing on. I could toss him a kindness now and then, but more than that would be meddling, and Fred Dolan had already told me what he thought about my meddling.

Joey's face was pimpled, and his teeth needed cleaning and filling. His nails were chewed to the grimy quick. His expression was vacant, but not with stupidity: he was empty because nothing had been offered to him, not even the suggestion that there were things he could get for himself. Every part of him cried out for attention that I had been forbidden to give. *Mind your own damned business,* Joey's stepfather had told me.

Most of the time, I did. Now I hoped the boy had sense enough to keep quiet about today's exception. I thought he would. Silence, so far, was Joey's one strong point.

We made it across Highway One without incident, both of us squinting into the mist for speeding tractor-trailers, which bore down without warning, and sighed as we trundled onto Main Street, past Arguello's General Store, the Masonic Temple, and Dietrich's garage. Swathed in mist, Pelican Rock resembled a child's toy village: a single church spire, a row of stores, a schoolhouse, the red brick Carnegie library. Wooden water towers jutted up from among the white clapboard houses, to collect the rainfall and store it against the dry season.

The town had been built a hundred years before by transplanted Maine lumberjacks, Portuguese fishermen, and wealthy seagoing entrepreneurs who made millions selling off the redwood forests. Here, on the wide and grassy bluff that extended into the Pacific, they put up replicas of the homesteads they left behind on that other rocky coast in Maine. They built peaked roofs and cupolas and gingerbread-rimmed porches, and covered the sides of their new castles with shingles shaped like the scales of fish. In these houses they installed huge cast-iron stoves, claw-footed bathtubs, and high-bred ladies whom they met and married on Nob Hill in San Francisco.

Accustomed to city society, the high-bred ladies were bored nearly to death. They formed, in short order, the Pelican Rock Improvement Club, the Needlework Guild, the Wednesday Afternoon Circulating Tea Club, the Association for the Preservation of Culture and the Dance, and the Pelican Rock Musical and Dramatic Reading Society, all of which survived into the present day.

At the same time they coaxed the menfolk into building the Congregational Church, also surviving, its white shingled spire piercing the blanket of mist as I drove down toward it. At last we pulled up in front of the Sea Gull, a low weathered-gray building with two entrances: one for the restaurant and one for the bar. We headed for the restaurant entrance, and I bought a Pelican Rock weekly *Lighthouse* from the honor box beside the door as we went in.

The Sea Gull restaurant smelled of coffee, bacon, and freshly baked apricot pies. Above the red leather booths, framed photographs of the town's logging days hung on the redwood paneling. Stereo speakers mounted near the ceiling provided Vivaldi's Four Seasons, to the accompaniment of clattering plates and the sizzle of the grill.

Joey surrounded an enormous breakfast of sausages, pancakes, orange juice, toast, and milk without much comment. I wondered what his parents would say about all the animal products and processed sugar I was feeding him; plenty, probably, if they took the trouble to find out.

At the counter, the men from the firehouse across the street drank coffee and gossiped with the barber, Bill McKenna. Two disappointed-looking tourists listened glumly, cameras still zipped in cases slung back over their suede safari jackets. With the visibility hovering around twenty feet, the local color this time of year was predominantly gray.

While Joey mopped syrup from his plate, I turned my attention to the *Lighthouse*. In it, the Coast General Hospital expressed gratitude for the success of the recent fund drive that had bought four new tires and a siren for the ambulance. Ellen Selander announced that her new gallery, Wavelength, would open May first, just in time for the tourist boom (the pair at the counter were out of season, as they had discovered).

Finally, a special town meeting would be held at four o'clock, January nineteenth, in the conference room upstairs from Arguello's, to discuss possible development of the Morris Cove tract.

Joey got up from the booth, mumbled thanks, and took off, promising to come and split wood in the afternoon. It was a school day, but I did not ask if he was going, since I did not care to become involved in the discussion that would inevitably follow.

I looked again at the paper, and back to the men arguing at the counter.

"The problem is we've got no tax base," McKenna said. "The tourists are paying for our roads and schools now, but what if the tourists go somewhere else?"

As if on cue, the safari-jacketed outlanders paid the check and left uneasily, their departure seeming to underline the barber's remark.

"So what?" Ted Bergeron was a thickset man, older than McKenna, with silver hair that McKenna had clipped very close to his big, blunt head. He clenched his fists on the dark wood counter and looked belligerently at the others.

"So we sell out to them?" he demanded. "At prices our own kids can't even pay? So we can buy sewers we wouldn't need if the tourists weren't here? Where's the sense in that?"

McKenna spoke up again. "Ted, we've got to build the sewers. It's not the tourists, it's the law. We can't just keep dumping it all in the ocean, screwing up the whole goddamn environment. It's a modern world, Ted, and we've got to go along with it."

"Yeah, yeah, well, the modern world can kiss my butt. We sell that land off to those developers, we're gonna have recreational vee-hicles up to our gee-dee you-know-whats."

He gulped the last of his coffee. "And when *that* happens, the tourists aren't going to think we're so gee-dee quaint anymore, and they *will* go somewhere else." With that, he left.

The rest of the men at the counter downed their coffee and went out with him: Ted and Bill and Hank and Milton, the Pelican Rock Morning Coffee and Argumentation Society. Each left a quarter on the counter and paid his check separately at the register.

As long as fellows like them survived, I thought, the town had a chance too. Pelican Rock was like a lot of small California coast settlements: lovely, and vulnerable. The people who lived here liked selling crafts and meals and rooms to the tourists, but now the tourists were beginning to want to buy the town itself, and they had money to pay for it. The locals were caught now in that time-honored economic bind: you can keep it, or you can sell it, but you can't do both.

The waitress cleared the coffee cups, sighing as she dropped the quarters into her apron pocket. Then she picked up the coffeepot and directed a questioning glance at me.

I shook my head. A line in the *Lighthouse* announced the Pelican Rock Writing Workshop at ten o'clock at the Pelican Rock Art Center, to be run by

published author Charlotte Kent, well known to all
and sundry in Pelican Rock.

Ah, fame. It was now nine-thirty. I supposed that
since it was in the paper and all, I ought to go. The
workshop was a paying gig, and as Bernie had kindly
managed to remind me, there was a rather intemper-
ate mortgage on my piece of the temperate forest; the
natives of Pelican Rock weren't the only ones who had
to decide what to sell, and what to keep.

Also, the students would be waiting to get back their
manuscripts.

I DROVE TOWARD THE ART CENTER with these objects
bulking ominously in the back seat.

Like *temperate* the word *manuscript* covers a mul-
titude of sins; to a real-estate lady, for example, *temperate* might mean anything that did not pose an active
hazard to shipping on the North Atlantic.

I thought that if I should ever spot one of these
"manuscripts" bobbing across the North Atlantic toward a ship I was on, I would put on a flotation de-
vice and jump overboard. As of now, however, I had
no such handy escape plan, so I pulled up and parked
in front of the Art Center.

It was a low, square, glass-and-redwood structure
built around the Hardwicke House, a Victorian sea-
captain's mansion that stood overlooking the ocean on
the last habitable piece of grassland before the cliffs.
Year by year, crevasses ate toward it across the bluffs,
which gradually were giving themselves up to the sea.
Someday the whole place would need to be jacked up
and moved.

For now, however, it hunkered beneath wind-bent
pines, the thermopanes of its newer section making a

tasteless contrast with the small leaded windows through which, in the old house, the Hardwicke women had watched for ships.

At the reception desk in the modern wing of the Center, Minnie Taylor presided over the cash register, a bronze antique specimen equipped with a crank in case of power failure. Minnie preferred the crank to the power.

The tourists from the Sea Gull had found their way here, and as they approached the counter with a few souvenir postcards, Minnie laid down the book she was reading: *Stilwell and the American Experience in China*. Accepting their money, she gave the register's crank an assertive yank, and the cash drawer opened with a rich *brring*.

The tourists were men in their fifties, dressed like department-store fashion models. But despite the modishness of their gear, their eyes expressed an old-fashioned motive as they cast what they supposed were secret glances at each other.

"I wonder..." one of them said, his finger casually tracing the design of leaves and vines on the cash register, "I don't suppose you'd like to get rid of this old clunker. It must be awfully inconvenient working on such an obsolete..."

His voice trailed off as Minnie fixed him in the invisible cross hairs of her gaze.

"No," she said quietly, "and I wouldn't have taken twenty-four dollars for Manhattan, either."

He had the good grace to look embarrassed, and after a moment, to laugh. Minnie smiled thinly in reply, as the pair left a business card for their antique shop in the city—"in case you change your mind"—and went out.

"Some people think they can buy anything," she said, shaking her head as she watched them go.

Minnie wore a navy silk dress, pearl necklace, and a navy felt cloche pulled down to one side. Her hair was short and thick and white; although she cut it herself with scissors it looked like the latest out of Paris. Her eyes twinkled sharply like little black buttons, and her skin was translucently white with bright rouge over the cheekbones.

"Well, Minnie," I said in an attempt to lighten her mood, "not everyone appreciates the past the way you do."

She smelled of lavender talc and looked at first glance as if she might crumble at a touch. A second glance, however, revealed her square shoulders, strong, erect carriage, and muscular wrists, all the result of a life full of plain food and hard work, upon which she thrived. I happened to know that before she came to the Center each morning she milked six goats, tended a garden, collected the eggs of four-dozen hens, fed and watered a hutchful of rabbits, and assembled the half-dozen apricot pies that the Sea Gull bought from her each day. Then, carrying the pie basket, she walked the three miles down Willits Road to her job at the Center, in order, she said, to get her exercise.

"Mmm," she said, unappeased. "Some things ought to be left alone, not sold off like so many odd lots of junk." She plumped herself spryly back onto the stool behind the counter and reopened her book. Then she smiled reminiscently.

"I sent them packing, though, didn't I? Teach them to try taking advantage of an old lady." Her chuckle sounded satisfied.

Her description of herself as an old lady was true enough, taken literally, but I did not think it entirely fair; to judge by what she did every day, she had energy enough for two twenty-year-olds. As if her other activities were not enough, she stopped on her way home every day at her friend Agnes Dietrich's house to set out doses of Agnes's numerous medicines. In her younger days, Minnie had been a practical nurse, and she kept her hand in with Agnes, who at eighty was getting a bit past figuring out her remedies alone.

Minnie herself was, I had calculated, well over seventy. Stiffening my resolution with thoughts of her example, I went on into the meeting room where the film club showed Bergman and Hitchcock on Friday nights, and where the writing-students now waited impatiently.

There were eight of them, two more than I had originally planned to take. But Marjorie Wickstrom was a local girl, fifteen years old and extremely talented, according to her English teacher. He had made several nervously insistent phone calls to persuade me, and upon reading her effort, I understood why.

Thin, pigtailed Marjorie had written a love poem in which the English teacher figured prominently. Entitled "Darling My Own," it rhymed and scanned perfectly and was also filled with the most determined sexual imagery I had ever read anywhere. Now Marjorie gazed at me with owlish incipient adoration through her thick horn-rims, from her seat at the back.

Of the other seven I knew only two. Kieran Gray was twentyish, tall, with blue eyes beneath dark brows and black hair that curled tight to his classically modeled head. He wore faded jeans, a black knitted shirt that strained across his broad chest, and leather-laced boots. He looked as if he ought to be out leaping faunlike from cliff to craggy cliff, seducing maidens and tootling bits of pagan song.

Unfortunately, his expression ruined the effect: as usual, Kieran looked as if he were spoiling for a fight. A familiar figure in town, he did odd jobs and delivered firewood, having dropped out of numerous English programs because no one in any of them understood what he was trying to do. This, I gathered, was the cause of his perpetual resentment.

His workshop submission, entitled "Untitled," consisted of forty pages of single-spaced dialogue between a man and, apparently, a dead rat. I had not known what to do with it, nor had I known what I ought to advise him to do with it. I knew what I wanted to tell him to do with it, but of course I could not put that in a critique, and at any rate the chance had now gone by.

With a smile that I hoped was at once reassuring and firm, I began returning the manuscripts, each with a paragraph from me clipped to the front.

The mood of the group chilled noticeably as eight pairs of eyes read through eight kindly worded comments. Then all eight turned to me, with expressions ranging from embarrassment to scorn, except for one pair of very wide blue eyes that read, blinked, and read again to make sure.

Emily Wetmore, mother of eight, was fat, fair, and forty. She wore a pair of powder-blue stretch pants, a double-knit sweater buttoned to her chins, and brown oxford shoes tied with plaid laces. Her argyle socks were mismatched, and too short.

Emily had written eight very clever double-dactyls, one for each of her children, capping them with a sonnet entitled "On Mothers" that was so lovely it had made me weep. In my critique I had said so, and at her timid request I had suggested markets for her work.

With one other exception it was the only honest encouragement I had been able to give any of them.

"Now, I realize that many of you will not like my remarks," I said.

Kieran muttered something that sounded like "you jerk."

"But you've spent good money for this class," I went on, "and it's my job to make sure you get something for it."

Kieran glared. Obviously what he wanted for his good money was praise, unstinting and unequivocal. He'd bought it; he'd paid for it. Now he felt cheated out of it.

"After all," I continued, "if I just said you were wonderful and didn't offer any suggestions for improvement, I wouldn't be helping you much, would I? You've come here to acquire further mastery of your craft, not meaningless flattery from me."

The phrase "mastery of your craft" mollified the rest somewhat, implying both future promotion and present membership.

Kieran scowled. Aside from praise, he probably craved introduction to an agent. In this, however, as in so much else, he was doomed to disappointment. Reading his stuff had been murder, but inflicting it on Bernie would be suicide.

Aside from Emily, the only bright spot here was Rena Blount, whom I knew fairly well. She had submitted a twenty-page proposal for a nonfiction historical book about Pelican Rock, with special attention to the town's architectural curiosities.

The idea was interesting and the proposal looked professional: double-spaced, carbon ribbon, wide margins, on good white standard-size bond. I asked the class to examine this work, as it represented acceptable manuscript preparation; in my critique, I'd made a few suggestions and said she might try it on a small California press, perhaps with sample photographs.

Now as her work was handed around, she flashed me a smile of smug triumph. "Charlotte, dear, you know I do appreciate your little remarks."

She simpered prettily and batted her lashes, looking adorable as always in snug jeans and a blue chambray shirt. A red scarf waved gaily at her collar, like a danger flag; small diamond solitaires flashed in her earlobes. Her short, wavy hair was the color of honey streaked with platinum, brushed back casually from her small perfect china-doll face.

"My little remarks," I repeated evenly.

"But I'm afraid," she went on, "that I'm going to have to disregard them."

"Really." I tipped my head in polite inquiry. It had been a mistake to let her in here. She would top any act, steal any stage, turn any and every bit of attention toward herself, no matter what.

And I had known it. And I had let her in anyway, despite the already too-large class. It was her talent: getting what she wanted. Any way.

"You see," she said, turning to the rest of the group, "the book's already been accepted. And my editor—"

She paused, savoring this phrase.

"—my *editor* thinks it needs hardly *any* changes."

Murmurs of mingled envy and congratulation greeted her announcement; at least, mine were mingled, although of course I tried to conceal this fact.

Rena wasn't fooled. She flashed another bold I've-beaten-you-at-your-own-game look at me, and went on.

"I just couldn't *stand* waiting," she said, "so I drove down to WestWorld Publishing. They pay such *wonderful* advances, you know," she added to me.

Grimly, I agreed that I did know.

"And it just *happens* that someone there is someone I used to know rather well, and he not only bought this book, he made a marvelous suggestion for what I should do next."

So, I thought, she hadn't even needed this class, and she had known it. All she'd really wanted was the chance to brag, to show herself off to the rest as someone who'd sold something.

"Hardwicke House!" she said, batting her lashes again. "And Dr. Stanley Edgar Hardwicke."

As the impact of her words sank in, I wanted to sit down. She wouldn't. She couldn't.

"This very building," she went on, "is packed with historical intrigue, which naturally is just what WestWorld is after. Something with punch, you see. Something to grab the readers."

These last remarks were directed my way, as apparently she felt I could use a little advice on the subject.

"Doctor Hardwicke was such an interesting man. He saved this whole town, in fact." Rena's look at me was gently pitying. "Of course, you wouldn't have known. Not many people do."

I bit my tongue. As it happened, I knew very well
the historical facts about Dr. Hardwicke. I knew, in
fact, considerably more than Rena did, but I didn't
want to tell her so. I did not want to give her the satisfaction of knowing that she had grabbed off a project I had been working on cautiously, secretly, for
months.

"*I,*" she announced, "am going to *reconstruct*
Hardwicke House, right down to the original furni-
ture. For the photographs, you know. Color plates.
Imagine, Doctor Hardwicke's actual bed!"

Marjorie glanced up, sensing something that might
interest her. The others smiled blankly—this had
nothing to do with them, after all—except for Kieran
Gray.

"All the furniture is in Agnes Dietrich's base-
ment," Rena went on, "and she's promised it to me
for the project. You know, Charlotte, when I went to
see her, she thought at first that I was you. Isn't that
the funniest thing? After all, you and I could hardly
be more different."

Hilarious, I thought, saying nothing.

"*And,*" she said, "I'm going to include some very
interesting information, things that have never been
told before." Her look was smug, as it always was
when she'd managed to dish up—or invent—some dirt
on someone.

"Stanley Hardwicke," she pronounced, "was not
the saint everyone pretends. In fact, quite the contrary."

Which was, as I also knew very well, perfectly ridiculous. Hardwicke had worked himself nearly into
his own grave, keeping other people out of theirs when
cholera struck just after the turn of the century. After

that he'd become a tragic figure, as his three young brides in a row met early ends: one by tuberculosis, one by a miscarriage, and one, the last, by an overdose of laudanum.

Their deaths made him into an ascetic celibate, his rigorous habits enforced by the fathers of eligible young ladies. Through no fault of his own, giving a daughter's hand to Hardwicke became equivalent to signing her death warrant. There even came to be a rude song about it:

Doctor, doctor, save my child
Fever's in her, high and wild,
Take her to your stony bed—
In the morning, she'll be dead!

All of this I'd gathered from old County Historical Society records, out-of-print California histories, and privately printed reminiscences. All of it, too, was perfect for my project: a biography of Stanley Hardwicke for the California Historical Society Chapbook Series.

For these, the Society paid a thousand dollars apiece. Big bucks it wasn't, but we ex-do-it-yourself-writers have got to start somewhere.

Nothing I'd found even hinted factual unpleasantness about Hardwicke, though, and Rena's remarks notwithstanding, I was sure there wasn't any. With her talent for gossip, the woman could make Mother Teresa look like a Mafia crime boss.

With the rest of her talents, she could also put together the deal for a glossy, expensively produced picture-book that would make mine look as if I'd scribbled it in thick crayon. In fact, it seemed she was going to.

Meanwhile, Kieran kept looking young, and envious, and desperately unhappy. Misguided or not, he just kept plugging; he'd been trying to write for years, I supposed.

Now here was Rena, grabbing the brass ring on her first try, and I felt a twinge of helpless sympathy for him. I could have told him that grabbing was her specialty; he wasn't the first person she'd infuriated.

Scraping his chair back, he stood and looked down at Rena, shaking his head.

"Sad," he said to her. "Like, you're really sad, you know?"

She gave him a look of mingled amusement and regret; it was as if a favored pet had suddenly got up on its hind legs to make critical remarks and so, of course, would have to be destroyed.

"Kieran," she said, "why don't you go off and do some of your menial little chores? It's much more entertaining to watch you chop wood than to read your...um, literary attempts, shall we call them?" Then she laughed, a high silvery sound, cruelly dismissive.

Kieran stiffened, and I thought for a moment she had finally gone too far. He opened his mouth to speak, thought better of it, and stalked out. Through the open door I caught a glimpse of Minnie frowning in at us. Then I turned my attention back to what remained of the class.

The time was nearly up, and going on was now pointless in any case; whatever mood there had been was broken. I apologized for the disturbance, invited them to come back next week, and watched as the students made their way from the room.

Several of them, the quietest ones, were probably gone for good. I hadn't asked to critique submissions before, thinking we'd better have a few in-class writing-exercises first so they could get to know me.

No sense, I'd thought, making them take criticism from a stranger. But these people weren't used to any criticism at all, and although I'd made my comments as gently as possible, the experience was too hard for some of them. And Rena's performance probably hadn't made them feel any better.

That was sad, but convenient nevertheless; it would bring the group down to the size I had wanted in the first place.

On the other hand, Emily Wetmore might not return, either; she didn't seem the type to listen to nonsense twice. Which would leave me with Marjorie, Rena, and, of course, Kieran.

He would come back. In me, he'd found what he loved best: an adversary.

Marjorie, too; she needed an object. I saw it in her eyes, beyond those thick lenses that seemed to intensify everything behind them, like burning-glasses in reverse. She would return, and she would be trouble, smoldering with repressed stuff and dying to tell.

Rena would ordinarily have been easiest to deal with. Forceful and energetic, she was already well on her way with her own plans. Indeed, Rena's own plans were the only ones she had ever cared anything about, and this came as no surprise. I was not her friend, although she ignored the fact, and although, at one time, I had been one.

Even so, I wasn't looking forward to becoming her enemy. Now that the shock of her announcement had worn off, I knew what I was going to have to do, and she wasn't going to like it.

Very simply, I would have to tell her. Not to try to talk her out of her project; she had as much right to work on Hardwicke House and its historical occupant as I did. But I did have a head start on her, and I thought it only fair that she should know.

More to the point, though, I had to establish that I wasn't stealing her idea. Not that I would ever completely convince her; my only proof consisted of notebooks and index cards, and although I could show her these I certainly wasn't about to let her read them.

Still, the longer I waited to tell her I was gathering Hardwicke material too, the angrier and more suspicious she would be when she finally did learn of it. Right now she was working on the assumption that Dr. Hardwicke was her private, personal property. Reluctantly, I supposed I had better disabuse her of that notion as quickly as possible.

"I'm going straight on home to work," she had remarked brightly as she went out. I decided that I would follow her there as soon as I summoned up the strength for the ordeal. It seemed best to have the discussion on her territory. Then, if things threatened to become too unpleasant, I could simply leave.

Musing over this, I turned to find that one of the other students still loitered. Elmer Wainwright was a tall, fattish fellow in his mid-thirties, with thinning blond hair, wire-rimmed glasses, and a sandy mustache. He wore rumpled slacks, a sweater-vest with most of the stitches raggedly pulled, and a stained, wrinkled tie with a bead of egg yolk centered like a stickpin on it.

Elmer had written a ghost story whose atmosphere was dank and chilly as the grave. Unfortunately its characters were all in various stages of decay, which accounted for a notable lack of action and suspense. His handshake was lifeless, too, and I dropped it as quickly as I could.

"My mother told me I ought to try this work-shop," Elmer said. "She says I should get out more. I guess she's right. But—I wanted to ask you something."

He fell silent as we passed Minnie Taylor, still perched behind the counter, glowering stonily into her book. No doubt what she'd overheard did not correspond with her idea of a proper writing workshop. I hardly blamed her; it didn't correspond with mine, either.

Elmer did not speak again until we were outside. Then he glanced sideways at me, like an overlarge child about to own up to a theft of candy.

"I don't make up my stories," he confessed. "I just write them. Is that cheating, do you think?"

"It depends." I turned my face into the mist, letting the cool moisture fall onto it. "Where do they come from?"

He stuck his hands into the pockets of his windbreaker and looked down, studying his shoes. I looked down also, and noticed that he wore no socks.

"My mother tells them. But it's not stealing. She wants me to write them, because she can't."

I shrugged, eager to be away.

"That seems all right. Is your mother..." I searched for a tactful way to ask if she were too ill, or too old, to write.

"She passed away, you see," Elmer said, "five years ago."

Hastily, I got into the car. In the drifting mist, his face was like a pink moon, glowing with delusion.

"Well, she won't be suing you for plagiarism, anyway," I said, and regretted it at once. Elmer wasn't really that crazy, just very lonely and odd because of it.

But he didn't seem offended. "Oh, no, she'll just be so pleased you think it's all right."

"Elmer," I said, "you tell your mother I said if it's all right with her, it's all right with me."

He smiled, nodding. The car rolled forward; glancing into my side-view mirror, I saw him wave.

Behind him rose Hardwicke House, its newer wing obscured at this angle by the moving branches of the pines. It was a tall white Victorian structure, heavy with garrets, widow's walk, crumbling cornices, and gingerbread trim.

Pulling away, I looked into the mirror a final time. But the light was shifting, and now in place of the house I saw the mirror itself, and the message on it, in small white letters along the edge of the rounded glass.

Caution, it said. *Objects viewed in this mirror may be closer than they appear.*

THREE

THE SEA GULL BAR resembled a cross between an overstocked antique shop and an Alexandrian bordello: dim and too full of beaded curtains, fringed lampshades, and oriental rugs. A hint of sandalwood incense hung in the still air, masking the standard bar smells of smoke and stale beer. In the corner, a pot-bellied stove crackled contentedly over its meal of sticks.

By contrast, Peter Ross looked sleek and up-to-date: clean lines, impeccable proportions. He wore blue cords, a wide leather belt that rode his hipbones, and a crisp white dress shirt with the collar open and the sleeves rolled up. He stood behind the bar, polishing glasses, pausing to pour me my usual as I slid onto a stool.

"So toss her out," he said when I told him about Rena. "If you can't stop her, you can stop helping her, at least."

"I'd love to. But she's still got the jump on me. I mean, she doesn't, but in her version of it, it'll look like she does."

I took a swallow of Irish coffee. "Besides, I can't get rid of her now. Aside from the way it would look, she's friends with Aaron Williams—that's how she got into the workshop in the first place. I toss her out, he tosses me out, and there goes a fifth of my income for this month."

Peter's expression made me want to kick myself; ordinarily, I knew better than to mention Williams, owner and director of the Pelican Rock Art Center, and buyer for its sales gallery.

As a painter of portraits, Peter understood about measuring one's income in fifths and eights and tenths; it was the way he measured his own. His shows in the city were infrequent but well received. His work hung in a couple of the smaller museums. When he was reviewed in the pages of a glossy art journal, the comments were favorable.

But good reviews do not a living make. Despite his successes Peter was by no means well established; in fact, he was poor. And meanwhile, Aaron Williams refused to show his work. Tourists, Williams had said, wouldn't buy portraits; who wanted a picture of someone they didn't even know? Now if Peter did seascapes, or harbor scenes, something the tourists could "relate to..."

At which point, Peter had begun to tell Williams what he thought Williams was related to, and by which sort of unnatural act he had been produced, and what Williams's mother had probably said, loudly and repeatedly, while it all went on.

That was why, this summer, Peter's work once again would not hang in the Art Center Gallery, although a half-dozen sales there could set him up for a year. He would rather tend bar for the rest of his life, he said, than sell out to that pompous schlock mogul.

Considering that my own most recent opus was entitled *A Heck of a Deck!*, I thought Peter's view somewhat unrealistic. Furthermore, Aaron Williams never bought schlock of any kind; he simply knew his customers, and if he said Peter's portraits wouldn't sell, then they probably wouldn't. But I never expressed this opinion; Peter's temper was at least equal to his talent, and he was sensitive on this subject. Luckily, he let my mention of Williams pass.

"You should have staked your claim earlier." He finished with the highball glasses and turned to the cash register. Ringing the drawer open, he began to balance the till, counting out tens and fives and ones into little piles.

"I guess you're right. But I was afraid it would kill the whole thing. You know how the old folks around here are—now that the tourists want everything, the people who've got it have gotten snooty. If they think *I* think anything worthwhile is up, they'll never tell me a word."

I finished my coffee. "Hell, that's another thing I hadn't thought of. Rena's so pushy, she'll queer my whole pitch before I get at those old characters. Good thing I've already started lining up interviews—I've got a couple set for this week. Maybe I can get to them before they hear about her. Damn it, why does she have to poke her nose in Hardwicke House, anyway?"

Peter cranked the new register tape around the spindle and closed the cash drawer.

"Great minds think alike," he suggested, pouring me another jolt of the double whammy.

I made a face at him.

"Or maybe they don't," he added.

"What's that supposed to mean?"

"It means maybe you should find out what she's got. If she's going to come down hard on the picture-book end of it, and just toss in a little historical mumbo jumbo for atmosphere..."

I shook my head. "She'd never tell me. Not if she thought I was really interested. You know Rena—on top of everything else, she's a tease."

Peter gave me a look of exasperated patience. "I wasn't suggesting you ask her, Charlotte. There must be a way to check it out. Find out how far along she's gotten, for one thing, and in which direction, for another."

"You mean her notes? You mean, *snoop* in them somehow?"

He shrugged. "Look, you've been working on the guy for half a year, now. Personally, I think the doc was a crock and I don't see what's the big fascination. But if you want to let her scoop you out of it..."

"I don't. He's mine. I don't want anyone to come out with *anything* on him—not until after I do. Besides..."

Besides, *what?* his look said.

I sighed. "Oh, I'm just wondering if maybe she really has got something new, that's all. Something I've missed. She sounded awfully sure of herself."

Peter looked skeptical. "Probably the old guy had an extra toe, or something. Big scandal."

I nodded. "Still, I want to talk to those old people, the ones who knew him. There's got to be more to Hardwicke than just what's in the library. That's what'll make my book good—not pretty pictures, but the flesh and blood story. Heck, everyone's got one."

I tipped the cup back again. Peter made good coffee, and he poured a heavy shot.

"I asked Minnie Taylor," I went on, "before I decided to do all the background research first. But she didn't seem to want to talk about him—I got the feeling she thought my asking at all was in poor taste, somehow.''

He poured me a final jolt of the Irish, thinning it just a little this time. I don't like to drink too much strong coffee, but it is hard to imagine what might constitute too much Irish Mist.

"Of course, Minnie's unusually tight with a story,'' I went on musingly. ''She never gossips—'what's past is past' and all that. But pretty soon all those old people are going to die, and if Rena screws it up so none of them will talk first—''

An awful thought struck me. ''Peter, what if she has got something? What if she really found something awful about Hardwicke, and after all my work I'll wind up finding it out from *her*.''

He shook his head. ''Uh-uh. Didn't you just tell me her whole Hardwicke thing was that editor's idea? The guy at WestWorld?''

"That's what she said.''

"So, she couldn't have had much time to follow up on it, could she?''

"I suppose not. Two weeks at most, and at her best she's no model of diligence. Besides, if she knew anything really juicy, she'd already be bragging about it— unless she thought she could create more sensation by keeping it a secret until her book's out.''

"More sensation, and more sales,'' Peter said. He picked up a paring knife and began to cut coin-sized slivers of peel from a lemon. ''So why don't you find out? Sneak a look, put your brain cells at ease.''

I shook my head. ''Sneak is right. I can't do that, Peter, I'm not the type.''

He gave me a knowing look. ''Oh, yes, you are. You can do it, all right. You're just not going to. Your trouble, Charlotte, is that the less you like someone, the guiltier you feel about it and the more fair you think you've got to be.''

He finished one lemon and picked up another. ''Now, Rena's just the other way. That woman thinks a scruple is an ancient Egyptian coin. She'll rip you off in a minute, if you let her.''

''I suppose you're right. All the more reason . . .''

Suddenly I'd had enough of Rena. I'd had enough Irish Mist, too. Just enough.

''Listen, do you feel like taking a break? I mean, seeing as I'm your only customer and all . . .''

His answering grin was delightfully predatory. ''You mean, get out of here for a little while?''

I shrugged. ''Not far out. Just a little ways. Like maybe, for a walk?''

His look was undeceived. ''Hmm. How are you at walking up stairs?''

It was just the question I was waiting for. ''I, sir, am the world's grand champion stairs-walker-upper. Of course, I usually have to lie down, afterward. And when I do that, I like company.''

He put down the knife and the lemon. ''Charlotte, I didn't know you cared.''

''I don't. I only want the fleeting illusion of male strength.''

''Yeah, yeah.'' He ducked from behind the bar, wiping his hands on a towel looped at his belt and locking the outside door. ''That's all I am to you. Just an object.''

''Of my affections,'' I said as we climbed the back stairs to the apartment where he lived above the Sea Gull. ''Besides, you're such a nice object.''

"Someday, though, you're going to discover the real me." He pulled down the patchwork quilt on his bed. "Then you'll be disappointed."

"You mean, under all that debonair charm you're a terrible person?"

He nodded. "Vastly terrible. Twisted psyche, raddled brain. You just haven't figured it out yet."

Nothing looked twisted from where I stood a few minutes later. Demurely, he pulled the sheet up to his waist.

I kicked off my sneakers and stood barefoot on the handwoven rag rug alongside Peter's brass bed. The curtains at his bedroom windows were also handwoven—shimmery raw silk of purple, green, and blue. An astrology chart worked in stained glass and set in a pecan-wood frame carved with suns and moons stood in the windowsill, transforming gray light to flashing jewels.

All of Peter's things were the same, as lovely as could be found, usually bought from local artisans: porcelain cups and plates, tapestry pillows, prints and paintings that had been made for sale to tourists but which he had snapped up before they reached the shops. They were, he said, simply too good to be sold for souvenirs; besides, he wanted them.

If Peter had not had such colorful taste in furnishings, or if he had not indulged it so often, I thought he would not be so often in money trouble. I thought also that the ounce of marijuana in the plastic bag on the antique oaken dresser was an extravagance, but I did not say so. Instead I hung my shirt and slacks on the quilt rack, slid in beside Peter, and tried to discover the real him. I gave it an honest, serious effort.

Knowing Peter was like being on first-name terms with the Rock of Gibraltar. When he said he would do something, he did it. When he said he would be somewhere, he was. And when he told you that you were the only woman he cared for, you probably were.

Not the only one he had ever cared for, perhaps; not the only one for whom he ever would. But, at least for the present moment, you knew the terrain whereupon you quakingly stood.

Or reclined, as the case might be.

By and by I had discovered as much of the real Peter as my nervous system could support.

"Well, was that the real you?"

Peter sighed. He always seemed a little stunned on these occasions, another fact about him that I found charming.

"Uh-huh," he said.

I looked up at his bedroom ceiling, upon which he had inked a perfect map of the constellations. The stars, just for now, had stopped in their dizzy flight.

"So far," I assured him, "no disappointment."

Now that I knew I would have to deal with Rena, I wanted it over with. But she wasn't answering her phone, so I drove home, instead, through weather that was shifting, the unsettled sky turning vicious as dark clouds mounted and the barometer dropped. Mist thickened slyly into bouts of rain, slapping down and subsiding. By evening, it was what the old-timers called "fixin' fer a squall."

Meanwhile, Joey had not kept his promise to come and split the stovewood. The bin on the porch contained only spiderwebs and splinters. I made a mental note to scold him for weaseling out of his commitment.

But the light in the shed was on. Through the gathering darkness, a yellow glow showed faintly from among the thrashing trees at the far end of the yard.

It was late for Joey to be working out there, in the improbable event that he was. More likely, I had forgotten to pull the string on the switch at some time or another.

"Ninki," I said, "go turn off that light." She yawned and turned her back instead.

That, in a nutshell, is the thing about cats. I grabbed my jacket and a flashlight and went out myself.

It was raining hard now, and the wind tore at my jacket and hair as I stepped off the porch step and onto a fat slug. At least, it had been fat. Now it was flat and stuck determinedly to my shoe. Dragging it through the sodden grass without success, I fought through the downpour to the shed.

Inside, all was peace. The sweet smell of redwood hung in the damp air. Rain pattered cozily on the roof. The sixty-watt bulb dangled from its cord, casting friendly rays of warm yellow light.

And I saw at once that I had been wrong; Joey had been here, splitting stovewood. The hammer and wedge leaned against the slab pile. A few of the slabs had been split in neat quarters.

Joey's green sweatband lay in the sawdust. I picked it up. Something was missing. Wedge, sledgehammer—axe.

No axe.

I shone the flash beam into the back recesses of the shed, where the pitched roof leaned down to meet the dirt floor. A gleam of red caught my eye: the axe handle. Scrambling in among the spiderwebs, I grasped it and pulled.

The polished head glinted, dull silvery blue. Something dark smeared its sharpened edge.

Outside, the wind picked up suddenly, rushing in the trees and rattling the shingles. A gust set the hanging bulb eerily swinging.

Back and forth it swung, in a short, smooth arc.

Back and forth. Back and forth. Then it went out.

"JOEY? *JOEY!*"

The storm roared above me, gathering speed, howling and lashing high branches together. The power had gone off in the house, too, probably along with the telephone. Lines down, I supposed, and the phone and lights were on the same poles out here.

I elbowed through to the Dolan compound, clawing in darkness at the wet leaves. It was just like Joey to hide the axe, once he'd done something stupid and injured himself. I had a good mind to let him take the consequences.

But I wasn't going to. His parents weren't home, and if I knew Joey, he could no more apply first aid than I could fly. He would probably faint if he saw two drops of his own blood; if he'd cut himself badly, he might faint anyway, all alone in that shack without any lights, with no way to call help. I couldn't just let him lie there and bleed to death, if he was hurt.

I pushed my way into the Dolan clearing, which looked and felt completely deserted. No smoke curled out of the leaning stovepipe. The shards of the windows reflected my flashlight, vacantly.

I aimed it into one of the junk cars. The fluttering cackle of nervous hens answered. The sound was oddly spooky, and all at once it occurred to me that anyone could be out here.

On the other hand, it was pouring harder by the minute. Unlikely, I told myself, for anyone to be lurking in the rain.

This thought proved less than reassuring as, mistrustfully, I regarded the house.

The door stood open perhaps six inches.

Anyone could be in there, too. Waiting.

For me.

I gave myself a hard mental shake.

Look here, my girl, there is a boy around here somewhere, and he may be hurt badly. Now, you can go help him. Or you can run home and hide under the bed.

Or maybe if you're lucky, some big strong man will come and save Joey, and save you from having to.

I looked around. No big strong men were in evidence.

The door creaked alarmingly as I eased it open wider.

"Joey?"

I didn't know why the hell I was whispering.

"Joey!"

The rising wind sounded muffled and distant from inside. I aimed the flash around the kitchen.

Dirty dishes, half-eaten food. The room smelled musty: sourdough and stopped drains. Ivy drooped in a planter on the sink. A poster curtly advised me to Be Here Now.

I took a step toward the hall. If he was in the house, he wasn't answering, which meant I'd better find him fast. If he'd passed out from loss of blood I'd have to get him up to Coast General, through the storm.

I took another step.

The door slammed behind me. The lights came back on all at once. The phone gave a startled little *ping!*

I jumped, then realized that the wind had shifted the lines back into contact. Quickly I searched the house, peering into the bathtub and under the beds, aware that the power could go off again any second.

It didn't, but Joey wasn't there. Wondering what the hell to do next—if anything; after all, he wasn't my kid—I went back outside. The storm had settled into a steady rhythm now, gray rain sheeting gustily across the yard.

I thought about the dwelling I had just left, and about his mother and stepfather, smoking pot and spewing rhetoric in some Mission District crash pad while the favored Liane lounged about looking beatific.

And I thought about the kid I wished I'd had, only life for me just hadn't turned out quite that way. I didn't want a genius, or a beauty; an ordinary kid would have done just fine. A kid like Joey, in fact. I felt a rush of fury against the absent Dolans; if he were mine, he wouldn't be out alone in the rain, in the middle of the damned night.

Then, drenched and shivering, I went home and called Deputy Sheriff Harold Flanders.

I hoped Harold would say something reassuring. I hoped he would know what to do about Joey. I hoped also that I would get him right away, before all the lines went down again completely and for good.

HAROLD WAS IN HIS FORTIES, tall and square-built; he wore faded powder-blue jeans, battered desert boots, and a sheepskin jacket. As deputy sheriff in Pelican

Rock, he took calls for rowdiness, drunks, vandalism, loud parties, stray dogs, and Fort Bragg teenagers doing motorcycle wheelies on the bluffs.

He broke up the occasional fist-fight, too, but only if the contestants were so unequal as to offend his sense of fair play; he disliked domestic quarrels especially, because, as he said, there was no sport in them. He dealt with the town's few bad apples by drinking and gossiping with them, getting them jobs on the county road crew, and generally demoralizing them into helpless good citizenship with his constant friendly scrutiny.

A few minutes after I called him, he was standing in my kitchen. "You know," he said, "just for once I thought I was going to get to have my heartburn in peace. That sister-in-law of mine makes the deadliest lasagna—"

"Bad, is it?"

"Hell, no," Harold said, "it's delicious. I had three helpings, and now I'm paying for them." He reached for my phone.

"Guess I better get on the horn," he went on, "get some guys rounded up. They'll be getting out here in about half an hour, and they're not going to be too happy, so be prepared. That Dolan kid is not the most popular boy in the country, and from what I've heard, his folks don't win any prizes, either."

"They're going to come out here right away?"

He looked surprised. "Course they are, Charlotte. This isn't Los Angeles, you know. Kid gets lost, maybe worse, we've got to start lookin', and from what you've told me, the sooner the better."

Of course he was right. We couldn't take any chances, so I hauled the big coffee urn from the attic, dusted it off, and began filling it with water from the bathroom, since of course the sink in the kitchen still did not work.

But now that I'd interrupted Harold's heartburn and summoned out a squad of men, I actually worried that Joey would show up on his own. Fifty or so local fellows would spend the night getting wet and tired, only to have his disappearance turn out to be just another one of his goofball stunts. I decided that if the searchers didn't wallop his bottom when he returned, I would find a way to take a couple of whacks at it myself.

The prospect cheered me only slightly. The coffee urn took sixty-four cups, which I had to carry from the bathroom in a saucepan, because I could not fit the urn under any of the taps and the shower sprayed at too high an angle. I had gotten thirty-six cups into it when the lights of the first pickup truck streamed into the driveway. Behind it came several more: cars and a jeep and at least one other pickup.

The storm kept up its battering assault all through the night as the crews tramped the woods around the house. Between trips with the saucepan, I watched from the window as their flashlight beams crisscrossed in the trees; their shouts came faintly, then not at all as the search widened.

By dawn, the rain was slacking off. A thin gray drizzle hung in the air like drifting smoke. They had covered several square miles but had found nothing to show that Joey was in the woods, or indeed, that he had ever been there. Still they kept looking, tramping doggedly, until around nine-fifteen, when a general alarm from Fort Bragg came over Will McKenna's

police band broadcaster. The call was for a fire at
Butler Lumber's Warehouse Number Six.

"Oh, Christ in a handcart," McKenna said, jumping for his radio to call in the volunteers. "It would be
Six. Just what we need—they got a million square feet
of plywood in there."

For the time being, at least, that put an abrupt end
to what had been, anyway, a fruitless search. It was
almost ten and the jeeps and pickup trucks were all
gone by the time I heard, through a haze of fatigue,
the Dolans' rattletrap Ford wheeze down the lane into
their yard.

Wishing that I had never heard of them or their
troublesome offspring, I hauled myself up and telephoned them.

As it turned out, I got an hour's reprieve. Harold
had been waiting for the Dolans, to question them
about their son, a process which sent Fred Dolan into
a state of high fury. He was still fuming when he came
over to my place, trailed by Phyliss and the wispy Liane.

"And I suppose you don't have any idea where he
is?" he demanded as, reluctantly, I let the three of
them in.

Fred wore a faded blue work-shirt, stained around
the armpits, and greasy jeans. The top of his head was
nearly bald, the remaining tonsure straggling out in
thinning ringlets. As if to compensate, he sported a
scruffy beard that resembled part of an Abe Lincoln
costume: I longed to yank it as he yammered, waving
his hands around like a cartoon character.

"Of course not." I sat them down at my kitchen table, which was littered with dirty cups and overflow-

ing ash trays. "If I knew, I'd tell the police. After all, he's a missing child."

I was fairly worried now, and so angry with Dolan that I wanted to alarm him. I thought he deserved a thorough scare. He was not, however, equipped to absorb one.

"Yeah. Oh, yeah," he said. "That's the way you deal with everything. Call the cops. Get the brown-shirts to kick down a few doors. Oh, you people are all alike, you don't give a shit as long as you're comfortable."

He ran stubby fingers back through the straggling curls of his hair, exposing the scar along the side of his forehead. A policeman had given it to him at a pro-test rally in Berkeley, where a financial institution had unwisely named itself "People's Bank." Fred's group had decided the bank ought to live up to its name and distribute its assets to the poor. The scar was now his proudest possession, demonstrating his firm opposition to banks, policemen, nightsticks, and other tools of the establishment.

He turned and stomped the length of my kitchen, then stomped back, aiming a stained finger at me. "What were you doing with the kid? That's what I wanna know. Buyin' him meals, tellin' him things, who the hell asked you? Who invited you to butt in? I told you before to mind your own business."

"Fredrick," Phyliss protested weakly. She slumped at the table, weeping. Behind her, draped against the kitchen counter like a vine in the last stages of root collapse, the lovely Liane nibbled her thumbnail and glanced at me in shy embarrassment.

She was only seventeen, beautiful despite her pallor and the starved-looking thinness of her face, but there were dark crescents beneath the enormous liquid eyes, and her skin was translucently pale, stretched over her cheekbones.

"Shut up, Phyliss," Fred said. "Bad enough the kid's a damn right-wing reactionary."

Phyliss blew her nose into a sodden wad of tissue. She had been pretty once, too, but now her features were quilted with fat. Her graying hair, skinned back from her forehead, was pinned in a haphazard topknot. In place of her usual bibbed overalls and sweatshirt, however, she wore a gold-braided purple caftan, a necklace of what looked like turquoise lumps, and huge hoop earrings of hammered gold. A Rolex watch cut into the flesh on one of her plump, grimy wrists; from the other dangled a gold bracelet festooned with charms.

Altogether she looked like the newly elected priestess of some bizarre but prosperous cargo cult, and I thought for once Fred's dealings, whatever they were, must have turned out well.

Under my scrutiny, she straightened; her tear-streaked face became sullenly petulant. "I don't understand what he was doing here, either," she said. "We moved the children up from the city to keep them away from unhealthy influences."

Her gaze roved behind me, lingering with disapproval on my bookshelves and on the TV, which didn't work anyway since no signals could penetrate our wilderness. I wondered if teaching her son to read would count as an unhealthy influence; from what I could tell, he only looked at the pictures in the Marvel comics.

"He was working off his breakfast," I said flatly. "After he practically shot his shotgun into the side of my car, which by the way I have asked you again and again to keep him from doing, I bought him breakfast because there was no food in your house.''

Phyliss had had another purpose, years ago, when she first came to Pelican Rock: to open a health-food restaurant in which she would serve foods she had grown and prepared herself. Freshly baked bread from stone-ground meal, organic vegetables, rich tasty soups flavored from her own herb garden—it was a good dream, and I thought a place like that would do well in tourist season. But the earth mother had gone to ground, now, her dream shrunken down to a filthy kitchen and a garden full of pot plants, weeds, and chicken dirt, and I felt sorry for her. I did, that is, when I wasn't furious with her for knuckling under to Fred.

"What are you talking about, no food? I left plenty of yogurt and tofu.''

Liane bit her lip and stared out the window into the trees beyond the yard, saying nothing. With those clouds of wavy auburn hair, and in her long gathered dress of tablecloth lace, she looked like the doomed heroine of a Gothic novel.

"You take him someplace,'' Fred said, "he's just embarrassing, now he's gotta go pull this.''

"Is that why you left him?''

Dolan frowned. "Huh?''

"The right-wing reactionary we're talking about is almost thirteen,'' I said. "You left him alone for three days and nights without any supervision, no numbers where he could reach you, no one to go to in an emergency, nothing at all.''

"Now wait just a goddamn—''

"Do you understand the phrase 'child neglect?' Do you know that if anything happens to Joey, you're responsible, it's your fault?"

"What the hell are you trying to pull? You're the one filled him full of ideas. I tell him he wants to write, just write. He don't need that spelling and grammar bullshit, that's for the bourgeois hacks. But no, that's not the way *Charlotte* does it."

Fred was, he thought, an accomplished writer himself, and so was qualified to comment. When he left here, I was certain, he would begin at once to compose an ill-spelled manifesto about how the slime dogs of capitalism had kidnapped his stepson out of my shed, after I'd primed the boy for brainwashing by feeding him murdered protein and denying him his twelve-year-old's right to carry a shotgun for his own defense.

"*Now* look," he went on. "Cops crawlin' up my ass, my wife's a mess, and for what? This is gonna screw me up but good, I can tell you. I can't go anywhere in the city now, I can't talk to anybody when I've got cops on my tail. And it's all your fault. The kid'll show up when he's ready. Why couldn't you mind your own damned business, huh? Answer me that?"

He stood before me, his hands on his hips, a fat little man with angry eyes and a foolish, belligerent face. Joey might be hurt somewhere, or he might even be dead, but all it meant to Fred was that he couldn't play with his underground friends anymore, now that the cops were taking an interest in his family.

"Screw me up but good," he repeated in injured tones. "Now what the hell am I gonna do?"

He was afraid, I realized suddenly, not for Joey but for himself. Afraid to lose face? Afraid that his buddies would find him too dangerous, and forget him? His whole personality seemed based on his status in what he called "the movement." If it moved away from him, I realized, it might destroy him.

I turned to Phyliss, instead. "Do you have any idea who Joey's friends are? Who he hangs out with?"

She sniffed and shook her head. "He doesn't have a lot of friends. He was always a solitary child, didn't like to bring his schoolmates home, even in the city."

Remembering the inside of the Dolan place, I thought I could understand why. I opened my mouth to ask if there were any relatives he might have gone to, but at a sudden, sharp gesture from Fred, she struggled up from the table, looking wretchedly beaten and resentful.

Fred's expression now was trapped and frantic, as if the full meaning of his predicament were only just dawning on him. Suddenly I wondered what kind of deal had gone so well for him in the city; what was it that made him so worried about any kind of official scrutiny? He could, I realized, be very useful to someone who wanted an errand boy: so insecure that he would do anything to assure his continued good standing. Weapons, stolen goods, drugs—it could be anything. Or nothing.

He pushed Phyliss ahead of him, glared back at me, then followed her and Liane out into the drizzle.

By now it was just after noon, and all I really wanted was to sleep. But Joey or no Joey, there was still a living to be made. Bernie's protests to the contrary, *Home Digest*'s accounting department apparently figured royalties according to a formula invented by Einstein. The faster my books sold, the more time it took *Home Digest* to write checks paying me for them.

Which meant that I needed an advance check, and for that I needed a new book. Even the Historical Society Chapbook Series was better than nothing. And I still wanted to talk to the old folks before Rena scared them off.

Probably, I thought, I would find Joey dawdling along the road somewhere—or someone would. He would show up, blinking vaguely, uncontrite about all the trouble he had caused.

Meanwhile, in half an hour I was due to interview two local ladies about a man who'd been dead for fifty years. Sighing, I began to wish I'd never heard of Stanley Hardwicke.

Still, a thousand bucks was a thousand bucks.

FOUR

THE JACKSON sisters had lived together in the house on Willits Road for fifty years, and they resembled each other so closely that if they had not been wearing different-colored housedresses I might have thought there was only one of them.

One, I thought, would have been enough. They were not hostile; on the contrary, they welcomed me with a stiff politeness that was as daunting as hostility, and less easy to manage.

"Sister," said Rose as she faced me stiff-backed from the narrow chintz settee, "pour our guest a cup of tea."

Beatrice looked at Rose, at me, and at the teapot, an ornate object of thin china patterned in roses and edged with fading lines of gold. With a defiant glance she leaned forward, poured, and replaced the teapot with an expressive *clink* on the silver tray.

"There," she said, and straightened again, folding her thin freckled hands in her aproned lap.

I had the feeling I'd interrupted a quarrel between them, although it was hard to see what they might differ over. Side by side on the settee, they resembled a couple of antique bookends: identically blue-rinsed hair, curled and sprayed into stiff bouffant helmets; identical dresses, one flowered blue and one green-sprigged.

They wore clip-on earrings, pinkish pearl clusters that I thought they had put on to increase the formality of the occasion, if that were possible, and identical cream-colored cable-knit cardigans with the sleeves pushed up, exposing forearms whose skin resembled freckled crepe paper. By contrast, their faces were remarkably smooth and fresh, each decorated with a little moué of pink lipstick. They looked to be no more than sixty-five or so.

"*She* asked us to help," Beatrice said.

I knew she meant Agnes Dietrich, Stanley Hardwicke's daughter and his only living relative. Two days earlier Agnes had called to say that the Jackson twins were finally willing to see me.

Just barely willing, I thought, as I took out my notebook.

"She's awfully senile, you know," Beatrice said.

I hadn't thought Agnes senile at all. But then, I hadn't seen her for weeks, only spoken to her on the telephone. She had sounded a little slurry, I realized now. And if she had mistaken Rena for me, as Rena had said, then perhaps Beatrice was right.

The thought only made me feel more urgent about the whole project, anxious to hear whatever old stories there were, before they got lost forever.

But first I had to deal with the Jackson sisters, who clearly did not want to cooperate and who had somehow been pressured or persuaded into doing so. Rose, particularly, was growing chillier and stiffer by the minute.

Something had put them entirely on their guard, and I was already afraid that I knew what. Or rather, who. Settling onto the rock-hard little armchair where they had put me, I opened my notebook to hurry the interview before they both clammed up completely.

"You're not the first to come digging the dirt on Doctor Hardwicke, you know," Beatrice said. "That other girl showed up, and I told her a thing or two." She sipped tea with an air of satisfaction.

Suspicions confirmed, I thought, sinking into gloom and trying not to show it. Rena had been here.

"Yes," Rose said, warning Beatrice. "You told *her* quite enough."

"Wanted to hear about scandals, she did. Anything juicy, she wanted to know. Fresh little thing. As if I'd tell—"

She paused as Rose looked sharply at her. "Even if there were anything to tell," she finished, seeming to come to herself all at once. "Which there isn't, of course."

"He came from the city," Rose put in. "Doctor Hardwicke, I mean. That explained a lot of things, his not being from here. He had a city way about him. Dressed like a London surgeon, he did, always the coat and hat and cane. Thought a good deal of himself. Which was quite all right, as long as things went smooth. But when the trouble came, he'd have done well to blend in a little more.

"When trouble comes," she said directly to me, "it's best not to be different."

"Yes, the trouble," I repeated, trying to sound encouraging without being too eager. They looked at each other, and a wordless communication passed between them. I could almost hear Rose telling her sister to keep her mouth shut this time.

Then she spoke to me again. "It was just a lot of filthy rumors. People had nothing better to do than talk, so they did."

"What about?" I asked, trying to sound uninterested as I turned a notebook page.

"Why, the girls, of course," Beatrice said.

"His wives, she means," Rose added swiftly. "Dying that way. Tragic, it was. Just terrible." She shook her head and looked darts at Beatrice.

"I suppose," I ventured, "people would have things to say about that."

Meanwhile, I didn't know what to think. I hadn't come to dig the dirt. I didn't really believe there was any, except in Rena Blount's mind. But Beatrice at least seemed determined to give me some. It was almost as if she were eager to tell me something, as if by talking about it she might get rid of it.

Only her sister's disapproval was holding her back, and now I was willing to bet Rose hadn't been here for Rena's visit, had only heard of it afterward from Beatrice. Rena had very likely gotten the whole, unedited version of some decades-old gossip, most likely untrue but still interesting.

Here, I thought, was where Rena had gotten her hint of scandal.

And here was where I wasn't going to get it, for Rose's thin nostrils now flared with indignation and distaste.

"No one said anything that needs repeating," she said, but Beatrice once again chimed eagerly in.

"The poor man buried three wives and that alone would have been enough, but . . ."

I thought Rose's black orthopedic shoe moved quickly against the stocking-clad ankle of Beatrice, but I could not be sure.

". . . And that was enough tragedy to start talk," Rose finished smoothly. "Some said he had bad luck, and some said considerably worse. It's all dead and buried now, no point in digging that up.''

Digging what up? I wanted to shake her. Instead, I tried another tack.

"I understand Doctor Hardwicke ran a sort of hospital in town," I said, smiling at both of them.

"He did." Rose sounded relieved at the change of subject. "For injured loggers, mostly. Horrible things happened out in the woods. And in those days a compound fracture was enough to kill a man. Gangrene. They died before they could get down into town. The camps were a few days out, you know, and they'd have to haul the poor fellow down through the woods tied onto an ox-cart. Then Doctor Hardwicke figured a way to save some of them."

"How did he do that?" I asked. "Save them, I mean."

"Well, it's not for a queasy stomach." Rose shuddered delicately. "You see, he used maggots."

"I see," I said, although I didn't.

"He used to raise houseflies in canning jars," Beatrice put in. "The men would take packets of maggots out to camp with them. Maggots, you see, will eat corrupt flesh. They cleansed the wound and prevented infection."

I sipped tea, considered taking a shortbread from the tray, decided not to.

"Of course, it made a messy chore when they got back, and it didn't always work," she went on with an oddly reminiscent smile.

I carefully refrained from imagining what the messy chore might have been, but Beatrice continued, ruining my efforts.

"It was hideous," she said, her voice rising. "The filthy creatures, like little white slugs. The wounds would be packed with them, and you couldn't be sure where they all went. They got in your clothes and under your shoes, you had to pick them out with tweezers and sometimes bits of flesh came with them—"

The look Rose gave her was pure poison. "You're getting carried away again, dear," she said, and Beatrice fell silent.

"To be so closely involved," I ventured, "you must have been—"

"Nurses," Rose said flatly. "And hard work it was, too, in those days. Sister likes to remember the glamorous parts."

I was as surprised as if a bookend had offered this bit of sarcasm; Beatrice stared miserably at the tea tray.

"We were both nurses," Rose said, "along with Minnie Taylor. Not exactly a respectable thing for a well-bred young girl to take up, either, back then. But what did it matter? It didn't, to us."

Beatrice cut in. "Because, you see, it was clear that we wouldn't ever marry. Too tall, too skinny, too ugly, and too poor. We didn't want the ones who would have us, did we, Sister? So we had to have work. Doctor Hardwicke trained us, and we worked in the sick house until the day it closed."

"You're grateful to him, then." I began to understand why Rose, at least, was so reluctant to talk about the good doctor. Who knew, she must be thinking, what kind of a book I might finally up and write, what buried ugliness I might resurrect for money?

Still, the hints kept coming.

"Grateful," Beatrice exclaimed with odd bitterness. "Of course we're grateful. How would we have lived, or gotten this house, or—"

This time the orthopedic shoe moved unmistakably. Beatrice winced and was silent again.

"He was good to us," Rose said. "The rooms alone were a welcome help to our poor budget."

"Rooms?" I said. "You mean, in Hardwicke House?"

"Good heavens, no. We lived in the sick house, Agnes's house now—the cottage in town. That was the hospital in those days, but he closed it before she married that German—by then he was too ill to keep up the work."

"I see," I said, although I didn't. One biographical fact I hadn't been able to learn about Stanley Hardwicke was what, exactly, he'd died of. "What illness did he have, if you don't mind telling me?"

Apparently they did. Their faces closed, flatly and abruptly. Rose's mouth made a thin, tight line; Beatrice stared at her black shoes and looked as if she might weep. The room's atmosphere dropped to the temperature of a freezer.

"He just got old," Rose said. "I'm afraid you'll have to excuse us now." Pointedly, she picked up the tea tray. "Sister is getting tired. I'll show you out."

I was tired, too. "I'm sorry," I said, getting up. "I didn't mean to invade your privacy."

"Now just sit here a minute," Rose told Beatrice, whose lip now quivered nearly uncontrollably. Then she walked me to the door.

"Just let it alone, can't you?" She glanced back into the hallway. "Let it be. You see how you've upset her, you and that other one."

Rena again. "But why?" I asked. "What can it possibly hurt now? All those years ago—"

She shushed me impatiently. "Now, listen. I'm telling you this for your own good. It's more than I care to say, no matter what fool idea Agnes Dietrich's got in her head. A book about Stanley Hardwicke, why, the very thought of it is foolish. He's dead, that's all, and it's better than he deserved."

Her face went hard. "He was a devil and a deceiver, and everything about him deserves to be dead and forgotten with him. Leave it, why don't you? Don't stir up sad memories."

She clamped her mouth shut, as if she'd told more than she'd meant to. Behind her in the parlor Beatrice was sobbing.

"We're old," Rose said. "Go away. Leave us alone." She shut the door.

Ah, the happy, carefree life of the free-lance writer, I thought as I hurried from the house. Striding between the massed rhododendrons around the doorstep, down the moss-grouted slate crazy-paving of the front walk, I wondered if perhaps I could get a job in a rivet factory somewhere. At least then I wouldn't spend my time making old ladies cry.

Reaching the lane, I glanced back. Rose still stood at the window, glowering at me. As I got into the car she shook her fist.

Thanks, I thought; I needed that.

And thanks to Rena, too. If she hadn't stirred them up first, I was sure this would have gone a lot better. Nothing bad could possibly come of such old gossip as those two possessed, if they really even had any.

But Rena would have gone after it anyway. Beatrice's hints were just the sort of stuff Rena liked. She gloried at even the hint of a blot on somebody's spotless reputation, and now she could snuffle after it shamelessly, with the excuse that it was research.

Cringing, I thought of her interrogating the two sisters, badgering them with all the tact and sensitivity of a dentist rooting out a stubborn molar. It was no wonder they'd gotten frightened. Rena was enough to frighten anyone.

In fact, I could think of only one good result from her clumsiness: it had put me in the perfect mood to see her and have it all out with her. I was just tired enough, just frustrated enough, and just furious enough to cut through her pure brass.

And never mind calling her first, either. I swung the car around toward her house.

SHE LIVED AT THE BEACH, in a low split-level of weathered cedar and triple-glazed panes. It was raining again as I pulled the Volkswagen into her sandy driveway. Despite Peter's advice, I had decided to lay my index cards on the table; in fact, I had them with me. She could do what she liked, but the idea had been mine first, and I wanted at least that much clear.

What else I would manage to make clear was a matter for unhappy speculation. Not a lot, probably. Rena took suggestions the way cats take medicine; poorly, if at all. Still, I was going to try. I tucked my packet of index cards and my notebook under my arm, dashed through pelting drops onto the deck, and rapped on the glass doors.

Like the rest of the windows, they were tinted to keep the furniture inside from fading. Typical of her, I thought, to care more for fabric than for the view; she couldn't own the view. Across the road, beyond pale dunes and wind-whipped beach grass, green waves slammed the rocks. Gulls clustered on the tops of the rocks, waiting for the rain to end.

I knocked again, huddled under the narrow overhang. The rain came down harder, solid sheets of it slanting across the sand. I knew she was here; her car was in the carport.

Probably she wouldn't like my coming out without notice. Probably she would even say so. Considering my errand, I wouldn't put it past her to start picking nits in my manners. Anything, I thought, to get the advantage.

But I didn't care what she thought about my manners. They were better than hers, any day, and furthermore I was getting wet. The glass doors slid easily as, calling out my presence, I let myself in.

Her spotless kitchen smelled faintly of lemon detergent. Cups and plates stood draining in the dish rack, beads of water still shimmering on the glasses. A damp sponge lay on the freshly wiped counter.

I called her name again; no answer. Then I went on through to the living area.

Plump pale sofas in mauve and lavender faced a pair of cream linen club chairs across the slate carpet, which gave off a pearly shimmer. Small bright objects flocked on glass tables: silver-framed photographs, china figurines, eggs of cut crystal, porcelain and jade. A trio of white birch logs lay on brass andirons on the fieldstone hearth, which looked to have been scrubbed out with a toothbrush.

Music drifted from upstairs; I followed the sound up the circular staircase and along the hall to her bedroom door.

The music was coming from in there: Sara Vaughan. In music, as in almost everything else, Rena had perfect taste; too bad, I thought, that Rena was such a perfect pain.

The door stood open a couple of inches. I rapped on the frame, hesitantly, because it had suddenly occurred to me that she might have someone with her. But there was no answer, only a moment of silence as the record-changer clicked and the needle came down again on Sara singing "Ill Wind." Feeling like a voyeur but needing to know if I should simply tiptoe away, I peeked in.

My first thought was that for such a careful housekeeper, she had an awfully messy bedroom. Then I realized what the mess was, exactly, spattered and splashed on the wall and clotting in the sheets.

Rena's bare foot stuck out from the bedclothes. It wasn't moving, and it didn't look as if it were going to.

I opened the door, trying to force some order into what I was seeing, but the essential wrongness of it kept confusing me. Moments passed while I tried to make the thing sprawled across the bed add up to Rena: foot, leg, arm...yes, right there ought to be, *had* to be...

I was looking for her face, but her face was gone. What remained of her mouth was full of blood. Masses of stuff stuck to the headboard: hair, and so on, glued there with gore.

I stumbled back. My foot snagged a loop of telephone wire and the phone came down with a jangling crash, the wicker table toppling with it. Books and papers cascaded to the carpet. I shook the tangled wire from my ankle and crawled on my hands and knees into the bathroom.

There I was sick.
Again.
And again.

FIFTEEN MINUTES LATER, I sat on the deck. The rain had passed. Salt wind scrubbed my cheeks. I thought it would take something rougher, though, to cleanse my eyes of what they had seen and were still seeing.

Steel wool, maybe. From around the curve in the road came the sound of an engine approaching.

I got up, but it was only Dawes Hobbs, in his blue panel truck with *Plumbing•Heating* in white script across the sides, heading toward town. As he reached the drive, he slowed, then turned left into the sandy track behind my car, stopped, and got out.

"Hi. Miz Blount around?" He ambled across the sand toward me, lugging his toolbox. He wore a gray sweatshirt, khaki pants, and a knitted green tam pulled down over one ear; the button on the tam read "IRA." His thinning brown hair was tied back in a pigtail fastened with a leather thong. From his belt loop dangled a key chain that held a rabbit's foot and a four-leaf clover pressed in clear plastic.

She sure is, I thought. All around. Something lurched in my midsection and I sat down again, breathing shallowly.

"No," I said, after a moment.

"Oh." He frowned up at the house. "She asked me to come fix her sink. You know when she'll be back?"

I shook my head numbly.

Shrugging, he mounted the steps. "Well, long as I'm here I might as well go on in and do it, save another trip. I hate to keep comin' way out off the beaten track for nothin'."

"Dawes, you can't."

He looked surprised. "Why not? Place locked up? I know where she leaves the back-door key. Otherwise that old leak's just gonna rot right through underneath the—"

"You can't go in, Dawes."

He looked almost belligerent now, with his toolbox in his hand, all the way out here and ready to work and not wanting to make the trip again.

"Because why?"

"Because she's dead. She's in there, dead. I called Harold Flanders, he's on his way, and I just don't think anybody ought go in and touch anything before Harold gets here."

"Dead?" Dawes pulled off his tam, his mouth hanging open as he digested this information. Then he quickly crossed himself, as if to keep away lurking ghosts.

"Hell's bells," he said. "You found her? That couldn't of been too nice."

"It wasn't."

The radio in his truck spat static. Dawes looked at it and shook his head. "Sometimes that ol' radio's more trouble'n it's worth," he said, and ambled across the sand toward it, pulling a small notebook from his pocket as he went.

I looked past him at Harold Flanders, coming around the curve now in what passed for a squad car: his own dark blue Dodge, with a red flashing light inside on the dashboard.

The car approached slowly. Harold was not the type to go screaming down the highway running his siren just to advertise his own importance.

After all, she was already dead. He eased the car onto the sand alongside the road, got out, and slammed the door.

"Hullo, Charlotte. Dawes." Hands in his pockets, he strolled toward us. Dawes came back to the deck as Harold climbed the steps.

"Inside, is she?" Harold asked.

"Yes. She is." Somehow saying it made it all come back, vivid and real. It could have been just a bad dream, except that if Harold was here it must be true.

He nodded consideringly, still examining the house, seeming to measure it with his eyes as if he were a prospective buyer.

"Better have a look at her," he said at last.

Reluctantly, I got up from the steps. Looking nervous, Dawes pulled the tam back on over his pigtail and picked up his toolbox.

"Not you, Dawes." Harold's voice was calm and slow. He was a head shorter than Dawes and twenty years older, and he smiled at Dawes in an easy way. "I think you'd better stay put."

Dawes nodded regretfully. "Guess you're right."

"You go along, now," Harold told him, "before that truck of yours gets hemmed in. Going to be a lot of people around pretty soon. We wouldn't want to tie up the town's star plumber."

Dawes grinned and loped off. When he opened the door of his truck I heard the CB radio crackle; he was a volunteer fireman, but he used the radio mostly for repair calls. He climbed into the cab and sat a moment, listening and writing on a small pad. Then he backed out, tires whining and spinning sand, and drove away.

Harold sighed. He had the face of an amiable bull-dog, except for his eyes, which were reassuringly calm and intelligent.

"I swear," he said, "sometimes I think that boy doesn't have two working brain cells to rub to-gether."

He glanced at his watch. It was an old gray metal Timex with a big scratch across the crystal, but on Harold it didn't look shabby, it looked right. Not flashy, just dependable.

"All the big shots'll be showing up pretty soon," he said. "You want to go in and get this over with before they get here, Charlotte?"

The thought of seeing it all again made me feel un-well.

"I'll stay here," I said. "You go ahead."

"Now, Charlotte," Harold said, "you know I'm not much fond of surprises."

I once heard somebody say that Harold Flanders could coax a pullet egg right back into the hen, and as I reluctantly walked with him back into Rena's clean and silent house, I almost believed it.

He raised his eyebrows at the mess in the upstairs hall, the table askew and the papers in heaps.

"That was me," I said as he stepped over them. "It wasn't like that. I sort of fell, and then...damn. Harold, I touched that stuff. I dropped all my cards and things, see, and then—"

"Never mind," Harold said softly. He had gotten a look through the bedroom door, at Rena. After a moment he turned, grim-faced, and went wordlessly back down the stairs.

"Did it occur to you," he asked, when we were back outside on the deck, "that whoever it was might still have been in there?"

In the distance, sirens screamed, rising and falling, getting closer. The beach road had been closed for weeks at the highway end, on account of a rockslide that Harold's bad-apple road crews had not yet gotten around to cleaning up. The squad cars and ambulance, I realized, would have to go on into town, then come around back.

"No," I managed to say. "No, it didn't occur to me."

"Didn't think so," he said, his voice stern. "Next time you go in someplace and find things out of line, you get on out. Don't poke around. You got that straight? Get on out and call the cops."

I nodded dumbly. Of course that hadn't occurred to me. I'd been so shocked by the fact and the manner of it all, I hadn't thought about who must have killed her. I hadn't thought that somewhere, perhaps very nearby, was some particular person who had murdered Rena Blount.

But, of course, some particular person had.

THE DISTRICT ATTORNEY arrived and said I would have to come to Fort Bragg to sign a statement. Yes, I told him: I would come, I would sign. Yes, I would testify at the inquest. The highway patrolmen asked questions, too, and so did the coroner and the reporters. There were four of them: one from Fort Bragg, one from the *Lighthouse*, and two local stringers from the city papers. They all asked the same questions, and I gave the same answers.

Yes, I had found her. No, I didn't have any idea who killed her. No, I didn't care to describe the condition of the body. No, there were no obscenities written in blood. No, she did not belong to any cults or groups that I knew of, except of course for the writing workshop.

Immediately I saw that volunteering this fact had been a mistake; the reporters began to clamor for the names of the other members, especially any who might "harbor grudges" or have "acted strangely," as they put it. They questioned me also as to whether, in my opinion, anyone's writings reflected "unusual states of mind."

It seemed to me that all the workshop members' writings reflected rather unusual states of mind; not, however, as unusual as the state Rena was in when I found her. As for grudges, plenty of people had their reasons for not liking Rena, but that didn't mean they'd do what had been done to her. As a matter of fact, I hadn't been feeling too cordial toward her, myself.

I did not tell the reporters any of this, however; instead, as I realized where their questions were leading, I began to say "no comment," mechanically and exhaustedly, over and over again until I realized they had all gone away.

In fact, no one was talking to me any more, not even Harold. He stood on the deck with Sheriff Bremer from Fort Bragg; Bremer had arrived a half hour after everyone else, in a squad car with the sirens screaming and the lights flashing. He had stalked across the sand with the air of a TV crime-show star and begun barking orders until he had everyone thoroughly confused. Now Harold was speaking to him quietly, with a calm smile on his face and his fists clenched behind him, as if they might get away and slug Bremer if he didn't keep them controlled.

After a moment Bremer nodded reluctantly and came over to where I was sitting.

"You're free to go now, Miss Kent," he said.

I looked in astonishment at Harold, whose face remained carefully expressionless except for a small twitch in the corner of his left eye.

He was furious. After a stunned moment so was I. It had not occurred to me that I might not be free to go.

"We'll be in touch," Bremer went on in grave, official tones. Harold moved casually up behind him. "We'd appreciate it if you'd keep yourself available. Keep us informed of your whereabouts."

His eyes tried to bore into mine. They got about as far as a termite in a steel mill; Bremer was a pompous fool, and everybody in the county knew it.

"Are you trying to tell me I'm a suspect? You think I might have done it? With what, my bare hands?"

He frowned importantly. "I don't think I'd care to comment on who is suspect and who isn't, at this point in time. Just stay available, please."

He moved away, head up, shoulders back, like someone about to be photographed for posterity.

"Harold, what the hell is he talking about?"

"Just off the top of my head," Harold said in careful, controlled tones, "I'd say he's probably talking about election day." He took a deep breath and let it out slowly. "But who knows? Even he doesn't know what he's talking about, most of the time. Don't worry about it."

"Oh, God. You mean he's going to pretend to be a real sheriff for all of this?"

"Yes," Harold said. "Nothing personal, though. He knows you didn't do it. The killer is probably two hundred miles away by now. Thank God," he added, massaging the twitch in his eye.

"How do you know that?"

"I don't, for sure." He pulled a small tin of aspirin from the pocket of his leather jacket, popped it open, and tossed three tablets into his mouth. I winced as he crunched them. "But there was a case like this in Ukiah," he went on, "two months ago, and another in Eureka. Before that, they had one in Sacramento."

I'd heard about them; everyone had. The Deadly Drifter, as the media called him, had been in all the papers, even the *Lighthouse*.

"So the thinking is," Harold went on, "that this is some drugged-out crazy guy, just hitting at random."

"But—nothing stolen, nothing disturbed? She was wearing diamond earrings, Harold, and a wristwatch that must have cost five hundred dollars . . ."

"Just like the others. The guy—if it is a guy—isn't after money. He's after blood." Harold sighed. "Anyway, if it's the same one, he's somebody else's problem by now. Well, guess I'd better catch up with Sheriff Bremer before he tries to tell the coroner how to do the autopsy." With that, he left me.

Clearly, I was expected to leave, too; just go on, I supposed, with whatever I had been doing before I happened upon the real center of attention, which of course was the corpse.

With some irritation I got into my car and backed out, swerving around the vans and patrol cars that clogged the narrow road along the beach. It was five o'clock and already pitch dark; my headlights plastered yellow disks on the streaming mist.

In town, I parked in front of Arguello's General Store and went in, choosing bread, milk, and cans of cat food from the packed, narrow aisle. A display of drain stoppers, bright red circles of floppy rubber, hung at the checkout counter.

That faucet, I thought, remembering my anger of the previous morning as if from an enormous distance, and while Rose Arguello rang up my order, I asked her about Dawes Hobbs.

"Oh, Dawes, he's all right." Rose's plump freckled hands moved competently over my purchases. "Better than those Wallerton boys—you know, they lay around in that shack of theirs until they run out of beer money, then they charge an arm and a leg to come down and twist one leaky pipe."

She handed me my change. "'Course, you want to watch him.''

"Watch him?"

She nodded. "See, Dawes likes to poke around. Look at things you might have put by. And then you know he's got a streak of the pack rat in him. But he's a good worker, and he don't charge too dear."

She looked levelly at me for an instant, having communicated all that was necessary about the local plumber who was a good worker and didn't charge too dear and was perhaps a bit of a sneak thief if you didn't watch him.

I thought I would call him anyway. While I am perfectly capable of buying plumbing parts and handling a pipe wrench, I know something else about home repair, too, which is that writing about it is a lot faster and easier than doing it.

I went home, ate some dinner, and fell into bed. The next morning when I woke up, I felt better.

But not a lot better: Joey was still missing, and Rena was still murdered.

Also, my doorbell and my telephone were ringing.

FIVE

FROM THE BEDROOM window I saw Liane Dolan standing on my front step, looking wide-awake and impatient as if she thought I surely ought to be up and about.

Harold Flanders, on the telephone, seemed to share this outrageous opinion. Rubbing sleep from my eyes, I told him to wait. Then I let Liane in and told her to wait. Then I picked up the kitchen extension and heard a familiar rumble coming out of it.

"Ninki, get away from there," I said.

The sound of purring went away from the receiver of the bedroom phone, and Harold began speaking. "Don't suppose the boy has showed up at your place, by any chance?"

There was a new sharpness in his voice and I knew at once that something unpleasant must have happened.

"No. Why? Has somebody found...something?"

Standing just inside the door, Liane looked anxious.

"Well," Harold said unhappily. "Well, I'm not sure. I got a call from Bremer a little while ago, though."

All at once I reversed completely my intention to wallop Joey; all I wanted was for him to be all right. If Harold didn't know whether he'd found the boy or not, that could only mean he had found something unidentifiable: something, I realized with growing dismay, that *might* be Joey...

"The weapon," Harold said. "The fellows found it on the rocks, out past the beach just below town."

I sat down. Liane was biting her lip, casting nervous glances at me.

Harold harrumphed. "Anyway, it's a shotgun. The murder weapon, they're pretty sure. And I happened to remember your mentioning a gun like that to me in connection with the boy."

I had asked Harold if there was anything I could do, short of swearing out a complaint. There hadn't been. Fred Dolan had a permit, and that was that.

"Yes, but Harold, there must be thousands of shotguns—"

"Single-barreled side-loading Winchester twelve-gauge with some fancy tooling on the stock. Couple initials scratched in the butt, J.D. That sound right?"

It did. Fred had given Joey hell when he scratched in those initials. It wasn't the defacement that bothered Fred; it was Joey's ideological error, his upstart presumption of such a thing as personal property. Fred did not hold with the notion of personal property, unless it was his own personal property.

"Yes," I said reluctantly. "That's Joey's."

"Mmmph," Harold said. "That's sort of too bad."

I agreed that it was, still not quite understanding.

Harrumph, harrumph. Harold was very unhappy. "Look, if the kid does turn up at your place, keep him there if you can. And call me right away without letting him know, if you can help it."

"Oh, Harold, come on now. You don't seriously believe—"

He cut me off. "Charlotte, I don't know what I believe. Because first I had a shotgun murder and now I've got a shotgun. First I had a psycho-killer drifter, and now I don't because it turns out that guy's already in jail, but I've got a missing kid. A kid who owned the murder weapon. This was all supposed to be somebody else's problem entirely, and now it's not, and I am by-damned if I know what the hell is going to happen next. So do me a favor and do what I say, okay?"

This was, for Harold, an unprecedented eruption, and it frightened me considerably. He was no longer looking for a missing and possibly injured child. He was hunting a murder suspect. I promised that I would follow his instructions absolutely, to the letter.

"There's something else," he said. "I took a ride back out to the beach this morning. Someone'd got into her house. After everybody official got done and left."

Now I understood his evil mood better. Sheriff Bremer wasn't going to be exactly happy with that news. And Harold knew exactly who Bremer would blame.

He seemed to read my thought. "I mean, this isn't exactly a major metropolitan area, Charlotte," he said. "It didn't occur to me to sit on her porch all night. We sealed it up. Somebody broke the seal. End of story."

"So why are you telling me?"

"Well, you knew her. I wondered if you could think of what someone might want. All the supposedly valuable things are still there, so unless they were just taking a gruesome tour..."

He paused hopefully.

"Sorry," I told him. "Kids, maybe, on a dare. If there's anything else, I don't know about it."

"Yeah," he said. "Kids. That's what I thought, too. Well, thanks anyway. And remember to call if you see the Dolan boy." He hung up.

I glanced at the clock: seven-thirty. In exactly two hours I had an appointment to interview Agnes Dietrich. By now I really didn't want to write the Hardwicke book any more; one look at what was left of my competitor on the project had taken the bloom off it, somehow.

On the other hand, if I gave up on everything I didn't feel like doing, I really would have to go work in that rivet factory...

Thinking bleakly of this, I turned to Liane, holding up a finger to keep her silent.

"I'm going to make coffee," I told her. "You can help drink it, or you can watch me drink it. In either case, you will not say a single word until after one whole cup has gotten into me. Understood?"

She nodded. A fragile smile twitched the corners of her lips. There was humor in her huge, dark eyes, resilience in the squared shoulders and the firm, faintly-cleft chin. She still clearly wanted to talk, but now that she had the promise of my attention she waited patiently and silently.

With some surprise, I began to think I might like her. I had always thought of her as a languid, passive creature, spoiled and favored over the lumpish, less-attractive Joey. Probably, I had thought, she read too much Elizabeth Barrett Browning and believed that looking terminally consumptive was somehow romantic.

I had been wrong. Liane was about as passive as a coiled spring. She waited until I set the steaming mugs on the table, then came briskly over and sat down across from me. We drank in silence until I asked her what was on her mind.

"Okay," she said. "First of all, let's get something straight. I've seen you staring at me, and I know what you think, but I'm not anorexic. I've got a thyroid problem, I saw my doctor in the city while we were down, and I've got some new medicine that's supposed to help. So don't get your bowels in an uproar over me, all right?"

I looked skeptically at her drawn, exhausted face.

"Yeah, yeah, I know," she said. "But it's just because I've been chasing after those two, Mom and Fred, trying to keep them out of trouble. I'm not sure it did any good, either. Sometimes I think I should start a reform school for juvenile delinquent parents—you wouldn't believe the crew they hang out with down there."

She sighed, and sipped coffee. "Anyway. I know that was Sheriff Flanders on the phone. He called our place about half an hour ago. He as much as said he and the other policemen think my brother killed that woman. Do you?"

I shook my head. Combined with her unexpectedly sensible manner, the coffee had the effect of a dose of smelling salts.

"Me either," Liane said. "He hasn't got the nerve, even if he could think of a reason, which I doubt he could."

Reluctantly, I nodded. "So where do you think he might be?" I asked.

"Maybe he saw something, or heard something, and got scared. He wouldn't take off for nothing—I think he's hiding. You know Joey, he's just a really backward kid. Even if they find him, he's going to try to run again, and that will just make everything look a whole lot worse."

She sipped again. "Unless," she said slowly, "you find him first."

"Me?" I set the mug down, staring at her. "Come on, how would I find him ahead of the police? And even if I did, what possible good—"

"You could talk to him," she interrupted. "He trusts you, you know. You're about the only one he does. And if you found him first, it would be a lot better for him. Don't you think so?"

Unwillingly, I conceded that I did.

"Because," she went on, "that's the part that really worries me. He's so hopeless, he might say anything. He might even confess to something if they scare him enough, if there's nobody around that he knows, to be on his side. You know he might."

"He'd have a lawyer," I said weakly.

She dismissed that one. "Lawyers," she said, shaking her head.

I didn't have an answer. I knew what she meant. I could just picture a lawyer trying to talk to Joey.

Liane watched me. I said nothing. Finally she shrugged, took a final swallow of her coffee, and got up from the table.

"Yeah, well. It's not your problem, is it? Anyway, I've got to get back. Fred's probably got Mom in hysterics again by now, and I'll have to try to cool her out. I'm sorry you had to go through all this trouble and all..."

She stopped. Her lip was trembling. "God, of course they would have to be acting like two big babies. And now here I am, acting like one, too. Real useful, huh?" She licked a tear from the corner of her mouth.

There was nothing babyish, I thought, in the look on her face. No girlish laughter, no giddy expectations. No hope, either—just anxiety and an awful, sick-looking fatigue. She was only a few years older than Joey, and she was wired up tighter than a guitar string. It wasn't fair; she was too young.

Also, she was right about Joey. He was a dumb kid, and it would be better if I found him.

"Okay, okay," I said. "You talked me into it. I'll take a look for him."

Her wan face brightened.

"I don't know if it'll do any good," I cautioned. "The police will certainly do anything I can possibly think of. But I do know him better than they do, maybe I can pick up a hint, or something. Anyway, I'll try."

"Thanks," she said. "Thanks an awful lot. I know it might not do any good, but . . . I just get so tired of being the only one worrying, you know? If I even think I'm not the only one doing that, it'll be a help."

I sent her on her way, thinking that Joey deserved something rather more useful than worry.

The question was, what?

I didn't like it that the gun had turned up when Joey still hadn't. Howard apparently thought he might have killed Rena with it, then tossed it and run.

I didn't. Knowing Joey, I thought it a lot more likely that someone had taken the gun away from him. Maybe they'd even taken him right along with it.

Maybe they'd thrown *him* away, and run . . .

This line of speculation was unpleasant enough to get me moving; after a fast sprint through the shower and into my clothes, I headed toward town.

PULLING INTO THE PARKING lot beside the post office in Pelican Rock, I encountered Martin McGregor, who worked for the *Lighthouse*, and who in his spare time wrote a column for it. The logo for this column, called "Pelican Pickings," was a fat, sly-eyed bird who held wriggling minnows of gossip in his great black bill.

With his plume of dyed black hair, his small sharp eyes, and an enormous wattle of flesh hanging down from his thrust-out chin, Martin McGregor resembled this greedy pelican, and I always took care not to let any minnows of information stray into his jaws. Today, however, it seemed I was going to have to do some judicious talking.

For one thing, Martin had followed me in and up to the post office window, where he trapped me between the counter and glass-fronted case of commemoratives. For another, Martin was the closest thing in town to a minister of information; if anyone had seen Joey Dolan before he vanished, or knew who had, it would be Martin, to whom every fact or rumor had worth, and a price.

At the counter, I waited helplessly while Jean Weston, the postmistress, peered through her bifocals at the return address on each of my envelopes as if making sure that it was all right for me to have them.

"Well, well, well," she said, her thinly plucked eyebrows arching as she peered at the final one. "Literary agent. Important correspondence, here."

There was nothing I could do about this; even in winter, Pelican Rock owned fewer post office boxes than it had legal residents, so that all my envelopes came to General Delivery. Jean claimed she was slow in handing them out because of arthritis in her hands; I suspected, however, that she just liked to give each bit of mail a last good looking-over before surrendering it.

She winked, tapping the envelope on the counter, gauging its weight. "Good thing the U-S-P-S didn't lose this one."

I took it from her hand, and she looked the tiniest bit affronted.

"No offense, Charlotte. You know, in a small town, people take an interest. Not like down in the cold, cruel city, hey?"

"Sorry, Jean," I said. "You know how it is when the creative mood strikes. We artists have just got to tolerate each other."

Jean's artistry consisted of a single work repeated again and again, a paint-by-number rendering of Jesus that she reproduced by the dozens and sold each year at her church bazaar. Appropriately for Jean, it was a copy of that painting where the eyes follow you wherever you stand.

"That's right, Charlotte," Martin put in. "That certainly is absolutely correct. I know when I've got a column due and no items to fill it up with, I get just as mean as a junkyard dog."

I ignored this interesting comparison and sorted through my letters: two bills, an advertisement from Magnin's, and an express letter from Bernie, apologizing for his hasty remarks and angling for a look at the new book. Finally there was a short stack of manila envelopes: the submissions for next week's writing workshop. I thanked Jean and tucked them under my arm, stuffing the smaller envelopes into my bag.

"By the way, Martin," I said carelessly as I turned to go, "you haven't seen Joey Dolan around, by any chance? His mom asked me to keep an eye out."

Martin looked surprised. "Haven't you heard? That boy's gone haywire. They're going to charge him with the murder. Frankly, Charlotte, I wasn't going to bring it up, on account of you finding her and all, on account of your feelings. Least said, soonest mended, you know. But now that you mention it, I wanted to ask you, just to ease my mind on the matter—"

He leaned toward me, his eyes fairly glittering with hungry interest.

"Least said, soonest mended," had never been his motto while I had known him. He had been heard to try "easing his mind" on subjects ranging from traumatic amputation in lumber mill machinery to the Congregational minister's oldest daughter's second abortion.

"Just to ease my mind," he would say to the mill victim's wife as Jean reluctantly handed over the envelope containing the compensation check, "was that arm cut off, or crushed, or just what did happen there?" His queries were so blunt and so unexpected that persons being questioned sometimes answered before they had time to think, which was, of course, the whole idea in the first place.

"You being on the spot, so to speak, I just wondered if she'd been—"

"So you didn't see him?" I interrupted.

Martin stopped short. "Well, yes, I did see him. But what I wanted to ask you, Charlotte, was—"

"When? Where was he when you saw him?"

He looked impatient. "Yesterday. Around noon, piling into some jalopy with some other boys. I told Harold Flanders all this already, Charlotte, he was by already. Terrible thing, terrible thing, a boy so young like that."

"Did you recognize the boys?"

"Well, of course I did, it's that same crew of drugstore cowboys that's always hanging around outside Swann's. I thought at the time the Dolan boy was too young to be fooling about with them. But they do get *ideas* awfully young these days, don't they?"

I agreed that they did. He went on before I could finish my sentence.

"Which was why I wanted to know if there was any evidence, if you don't mind my mentioning what you might call an indelicate topic, anything you saw that made you think she might have been, uh, you know, interfered with. Personally, that is."

I just kept looking at him.

"Because, you see," he went on, looking extremely uncomfortable as if he knew that he had gone too far, even for a collector of pelican pickings, "people will talk, as you must know.

"And," he went on, "I feel it's my duty to set them straight, whenever I can. Put the lid on some of the wilder stories, you might say."

I happened to know that Martin's habit, when he got hold of the wilder stories, was to spread them around like rice at a wedding. He loved gossip, the racier the better, and I took a faintly malicious pleasure in laying this particular bit of it to rest.

"I don't think there was anything like that," I told him. "If people come around saying there was, you can just tell them I said it's not true."

"Oh." He tried to look relieved, and failed. "All right then, Charlotte. I'm glad we got that straightened out right away."

"Me too," I said, on my way out. He wasn't glad, but of course he couldn't very well say so. Still, he'd gotten an answer to his question, and I'd gotten an answer to mine.

"NAH, WE DIDN'T GO," Billy Upson said.

He was thirteen or so, and with his pals he leaned against the redwood planter in front of Swann's, trying to look tough. He was like a miniature negative of his father, with the same blunt head, square jaw, and pug nose, but where Ted Upson was fair and plain, the boy was darker and had a sly, pointy cast to his face. He wore a denim jacket and jeans, square-toed leather boots, and a spiked leather wristlet which I suspected his father didn't know he owned.

"Whadda we wanna hang out with that bunch for?" the Upson boy asked rhetorically, and his buddies nodded.

I recognized the Wallace twins, blond and gangly with identical Adam's apples bobbing in tandem; between them stood Bobby Stawicki, gnawing a cuticle and eyeing me suspiciously. John Mendillo, a bit apart from the rest, was the only one who did not look as if he expected trouble from me, and when the others fell silent, he spoke up.

"Joey went with Kenny Biewald. I saw him, I saw him get into the car. I was across the street, working in the store." He shook his head. "You guys, you're gonna get in trouble. You ought to of told Mister Flanders he went.''

''Shut up, Mendillo,'' Billy said. ''Just shut up. You're the one in trouble.''

''I am not,'' John said stoutly. ''That Ken Biewald, he's a jerk. You guys're scared of him 'cause he's got a gang. Big deal. Now you went and lied to Mister Flanders, and you're gonna get it.''

''Wait a minute,'' I said. ''How old is this Biewald kid, anyway?''

''Seventeen.'' The Stawicki boy looked nervous. ''And so are his friends. And they don't like guys who talk about 'em.''

''But Joey's only twelve. What would a big boy like that want with Joey?''

Billy Upson laughed unpleasantly. ''Maybe Joey's got something he wants.''

The others looked at each other slyly. ''Yeah, we shoulda thought of that,'' said one of the Wallace boys.

''Thought of what?''

''Oh, nothin','' Billy Upson said, turning away. I reached out and plucked the joint he had inexpertly concealed from his shirt pocket.

''Hey! Gimme that!'' He turned and grabbed for it; I dropped it on the sidewalk and ground my heal on it.

''Very interesting,'' I told him. ''You should be more careful. And you should be very careful how you talk to me, Billy, because I know your father. And I also know Harold Flanders, and between the two of them they can make your life miserable.''

Billy bit his lip and looked past me.

''Now,'' I said, ''what did the Biewald boy want with Joey?''

"That." Billy aimed a grubby finger at the ruined joint.

I blinked. "Dope? He thought he could get it from Joey?"

"Everybody knows his dad's some kind of big crook," John Mendillo said. "He was in jail, and everything."

"Yeah," one of the Wallace boys chimed in, "an' everybody knows what he went there for."

I didn't know. "What?"

"Drugs," Billy said. "He was a dealer. God, you've got to be pretty stupid not to know that."

I'd have liked to ask the boys more because suddenly I remembered the bag of pot I'd seen on Peter's dresser. It hadn't occurred to me then to wonder where he'd gotten it, but I did now.

Just how much went on around here, I thought, that I didn't know anything about?

"I'VE TAKEN THOSE," said Agnes Dietrich, and clamped her lips together stubbornly.

The parlor of her cottage on Pine Street was furnished with fragile-looking armchairs upholstered in pale silk, their high backs, straight arms, and shallow seats reminding me of a school for young ladies that I had once, briefly, attended.

"That was yesterday, dear, remember? These are your pills for today. See?" Minnie Taylor's voice was a practiced mixture of coaxing and firmness as she set the bottles and jars on a tray before Agnes.

She spoke to me in a low aside. "It's good that you came now. She's not what she was. I've had to start coming by in the mornings too. Don't take too much notice of her wanderings, will you?"

She poured a shotglass full of fluid the color of old port. "And here is your tonic. Those others are your heart pill, and blood pressure pills, and the settler for your nerves."

Minnie had been coming up from the cellar as I arrived, since it was her habit every day to check the whole house and make sure everything was as it should be. Now she put each dose of medicine into a small separate plastic cup and lined the cups on the TV tray in front of Agnes, who sat swathed in shawls in a blue velvet armchair.

It was easy to see, I thought, why Agnes Dietrich was as fragile-looking as old porcelain; with all those medicines inside her, she probably had no room for food.

"Hmmph," she said, eyeing the cups suspiciously from under lids that were heavy and wrinkled, like old draperies. Then, slowly, she began to swallow the pills, her blue-veined hand moving with slow care from the table to her shriveled mouth and back again.

An elaborate brass fireplace fan stood to one side of the tiled hearth; hand-painted blue-and-white Meissen designs adorned the tiles, and on the polished andirons a skillful construction of kindling and seasoned, split redwood logs had been recently set ablaze. There was no sound from the rest of the house, which smelled of mothballs, lavender, and Constant Comment tea.

"That's right, Agnes," Minnie said, watching her charge approvingly. "And when you've finished, you have a visitor. Charlotte Kent is here. You remember Charlotte."

The heavy eyelids flickered in my direction. "Hmmph," Agnes said again, and took another pill.

I lowered myself to the seat of a slender sofa whose tufted upholstery was the color of old wine. With its slim turned legs and its scrolled armrests winging out at oblique angles, it seemed barely sturdy enough to hold its own weight, much less mine, but it bore me without complaint.

The fire blazed pleasantly but gave off little heat. While Agnes took her doses, I finished my inspection of the Turkish carpet and the lamps, which were either real Tiffanys or very good imitations, and turned my attention to the series of oil portraits that hung, in the old-fashioned way, by tasseled cords from the trim of the ornate woodwork.

Meanwhile, Minnie hovered about. "That's Doctor Hardwicke," she said as she saw me examining a painting of a bearded man in a morning coat.

His gaze was piercing, his forehead high and intelligent. The painter had given him graceful hands, pink and youthful skin, and a mouth whose full redness betrayed a knowledge of passion despite unfortunate experience.

All those wives, I thought, as Agnes managed at last to down the final pill.

"Very good," Minnie Taylor said. She gathered the medicine bottles and the tonic jar, and put them into an inlaid cabinet to one side of the tiled hearth. "Why, my goodness, I see I'm not due at the Center for half an hour. You don't mind if I just sit here a bit, do you? I'll be quiet as a mouse."

Her shiny-button eyes gave Agnes a once-over; then, with a satisfied nod, she settled down to her book. In the hall, I heard Milton Dietrich, Agnes's son, as he went off to his work: Dietrich's Garage, Milton Dietrich, Prop.

"You're not that girl," Agnes said abruptly.

"No, I'm not Rena," I said, thinking, *her again*.

"Hmmph. All you young ones look alike. Just as well you aren't her, too, isn't it?"

I said that it was.

"I get confused, you know."

I said I did. Minnie glanced up, then went back to her reading.

Agnes poured tea with a shaking hand, gestured at me to do the same, and slurped the hot liquid thirstily. "Damned medicines dry my mouth up."

I nodded, not knowing what to say. The change in Agnes since I'd seen her last was shocking. Only a few weeks ago she'd been a sharp, vigorous woman; now her eyes resembled a chipmunk's, bright but only half comprehending. I forced myself to remember that she was past eighty—considerably past.

"I needed money," she said. "That's why I told her she could have the furniture. She offered a fee. They're robbing me blind, you know, and I needed the money."

This was nonsense. The Art Center paid her a rent on Hardwicke House, in addition to the sum she received each month from the trust that had been set up for her. Whatever else Stanley Hardwicke had been, he had been a shrewd manager and had hired good lawyers. I gathered they had gradually taken over his financial affairs, investing his money and paying his bills. In any case, Agnes was not poor and was not about to become so.

Rena, no doubt, had played on her fantasies nevertheless. I wondered how much she had offered, but by reputation at least, I knew Agnes better than to think she would ever tell. Even in her younger days, word had it that she'd been shrewd, suspicious, and compulsively tight with a penny. Now, in addition, she had developed a morbid fear of being packed off to an institution.

She wore, in this chilly house, an odd collection of layers: a pink suit-skirt I had seen before; heavy stockings in black lacy wool; a cardigan whose plain hand-knit pattern set off nicely the pale yellow yarn, slightly iridescent, of which it was made. I thought that underneath these layers she probably wore long underwear; her manner said plainly that she could do, and wear, whatever she damn well pleased.

Or at least, what remained of her manner said so. As I watched, she dug among the folds of her crocheted lap robe, produced a lighter and a crumpled pack of unfiltered cigarettes, withdrew one, and peered suspiciously at it for several seconds.

Then she lit it. "So, girl. What do you want from me?"

Indeed, I thought. She had teased me for weeks with phone calls, questions, and suggestions, making and breaking dates for interviews like some coy debutante. At the time, I'd been furious.

Now, though, I thought she might have been getting confused even then. And Rena had played on that confusion to get promises from her and to get through her to the Jackson sisters. I felt a burst of fury at the dead woman: she would use anything.

Still, there was no point being angry about it now. I hoisted my bag and pulled out my notebook.

"I'd like an idea of the background," I began. "What, for example, you hope to gain from helping me get the book written."

Agnes grinned, smoke wafting from behind her false teeth. The effect was dreadful.

"Revenge," she said clearly. Out of the corner of my eye, I saw Minnie's head come up. Then, catching my glance, she looked down again.

I looked down, too. The notebook lay open in my lap.

I blinked, then stared at it.

"Revenge," Agnes repeated. Her bright eyes sparkled with sudden wickedness. "I've waited a long, long time. And no one will stop me now."

I thought this remark seemed directed at Minnie but couldn't be sure. In fact, at the moment I didn't feel I could be sure of anything.

The notebook in my lap was not mine.

Agnes nodded, her wrinkled lips pressed tight.

"Talk, you know," she said. "Evil, evil talk. All the neighbors, turning the other way."

"Is something wrong, dear?" Minnie said to me.

"Oh, no," I said brightly, forcing a smile. "Just . . . finding a clean page. I *must* get organized."

Also, I must think of something sensible to say. On the page in my lap, three names were written: Eliza Tate. Margaret Walsh. Cordelia Upson.

Not in my handwriting, though. In Rena's.

"But I should think," I said haltingly to Agnes, trying to compose myself, "I should think by now you'd lived past concern for your neighbor's opinions."

What the hell was Rena's notebook doing here?

Agnes cocked me a cool, amused look, seeming to notice my confusion. And how do *you* like it, her expression seemed to say.

"Would you, now? Would you think that?" Her eyelids lowered; for a moment I was afraid she might drift off to sleep. Instead she sighed, and frowned consideringly at the cigarette.

I flipped pages: lists of furniture; diagrams of rooms; scribbled reminder to buy film, ASA 400. All in Rena's writing, not my own.

Because the book only looked like mine: spiral bound, green cardboard covers, plastic tabs to mark the sections. And that was how I had mistaken it.

That was how, in my shock and in the confusion of scattered papers outside Rena's bedroom, I had thought it was mine and gathered it up with dropped papers of my own.

"Doctor Hardwicke," Agnes said. The words came twisting out of her mouth; she ground the cigarette into a shell-pink porcelain tray. "An ordinary man. Lived a plain life, did his duty. They hounded him for it. And they ought to pay."

"Hounded?" I tried to look as if I were paying attention. But through my own dismay, I saw already that I wouldn't get much useful information out of Agnes.

Meanwhile, on the last written-on page of the notebook, I found: $C_{17}H_{21}O_4NHCl$. A chemical formula; a drug or medicine of some sort?

"He nursed their daughters," Agnes insisted, getting up steam as she talked. "They ought to have thanked him. Cared for them until they died, and then they blamed him. Was it his fault the girls' veins ran skim milk?"

She glared demandingly at me; Minnie looked uneasy.

"Was it his fault," Agnes said, spots of color appearing in her cheeks, "that they never got any fresh air, never took off the whalebone corsets that pressed their vitals to death? He loved them, he did. Took care of them. But they died. People do, you know!"

She finished furiously, leaning forward in her chair as if to make sure that I too recognized this hard fact.

Looking at her, I recognized it only too well.

"That must have been hard for you," I said placatingly, doing quick mental arithmetic and wishing very much that I hadn't come. "You were what, twelve years old when your mother died?"

She looked contradictingly at me, as if she thought I'd changed the subject. Then after a moment she assented in a grudging tone. "Corintha. My mother's name was Corintha. Then Evelina. I was fourteen when Evelina went."

"And the third one, the one who took laudanum—"

"She was wrongheaded before he got to her, bound for the grave before he brought her into the house. She used to dress up in black lace and crepe and wander the upstairs, moaning and calling—"

"And her name," I persisted, hating myself for it. But she might still have a few recallable nuggets of fact, things no one else knew. If she did, they would soon be gone forever.

"What was her name?" I asked again. I knew it, but I wanted to know how much she was remembering and how much she made up.

Meanwhile, the notebook lay in my lap like an alien thing.

"Leonora," she said, leaning back. "He loved her more than all the rest. They'd been married three months. To him she was the sun and the moon and the stars. But she swallowed poison and died in his arms."

"Why? Why would she do that?"

She gave me a glance that suggested I was very stupid.

"Because she was mad. I told you. She came to the surgery wanting drugs to settle her mind. He fell in love with her. He wasn't smart about females, you see." She glanced at the portrait, at that passionate, repressed face. "I say that, although he was my father, because it was true. He simply loved women."

Loved them to death, I thought irreverently. Minnie Taylor got up from her chair and began to bustle about the room, casting meaningful frowns at me. I supposed it wouldn't make her job easier, my getting Agnes all worked up.

"Leonora Crusoe," Agnes said, "put the last nail in his coffin. At the end even she'd turned against him, you see. Mad."

"And after that?" *Just a few more minutes,* I thought at Minnie. Now that her mind was turned toward the distant past, Agnes seemed much clearer. If only, I thought, I'd gotten to her a few weeks ago.

"I married Dietrich," she said. "He went in the woods. A log fell on him, and he died."

It seemed a brisk and coldhearted summary of a marriage that had managed to produce a child.

"How did your father get on without you?"

He must, I imagined, have gotten used to the presence of a convenient spinster, especially with that succession of invalids to nurse. At twenty-five, Agnes Hardwicke would have been thought well past marrying age. But then, Dietrich was a German name;

immigrant laborers would not have been so discriminating in their choice of wives.

"His nurses took care of him. The Jacksons, and Minnie. Finally he died himself, of...of a broken heart."

She glanced at me, to see how I took this, and for just an instant her look was sly.

Lying, I thought. There was something else, something she was daring me to find out. Men have died, and worms have eaten them, but not for love.

She spoke again. "He never stopped grieving for Leonora. That was the beginning of it, when he said he heard her voice in the house, calling and crying. I thought of hiring him an attendant, some man strong enough to restrain him, but then of course it wasn't necessary."

"He needed restraint?"

She frowned. "He was...difficult. That much was true. He accused people of things they could not possibly have done. He needed humoring, that was all. But the people he'd saved in the cholera time wanted him put away, and in those days the madhouse was even worse than now. A living death. But he cheated them. He saved himself from that last humiliation. Saved himself from a town full of vicious fools."

Throughout this recitation she held her teacup a few inches from her lips, her eyes fixed distantly on that sad spectacle of long ago, as real to her, as bitter a pain as if it were happening this moment.

If it had happened at all.

"No one wants to talk about it now," she said. "No one wants to remember that they were cruel."

I began to understand why she had seized on my notion of a book. It sounded as if, real or fantasy, she'd been nursing this grudge for sixty years.

"And you want me to tell the story of that part of his life," I said slowly, "the part no one talks about. Make it all real again, just as it was, and set it right. Is that it?"

"Yes!" She set the cup so sharply on the tray, I thought it would break, but like the woman who held it, the translucent china was not as fragile as it looked.

She gazed at the portrait. "My father suffered enough for this town. He gave his life to it. And then they said he killed those girls, and they tortured him for it, hounded him to death. I want his memory cleared, I want him shown for what he was—a good man. He died of bad luck and cruelty. I want that cruelty exposed, I want it convicted."

I followed her stare. Stanley Hardwicke gazed mildly down out of the painting, one shapely hand resting on a large, leather-bound book. Behind him the artist had painted a window, and through the drawn-back crimson draperies I saw the ocean of all those years ago, a pastel sky, and the suggestion of a ship. The representation was serene, yet the shadow of spoilage was already in it: the hint of voluptuous appetite in the rich, red fabrics; the feminine hand; the haughtiness half-concealed in the bland expression.

Beatrice Jackson's words came back to me: *buried three wives, and that was enough to start talk*...

I began to wonder how much of a scandal those dead wives had really been, and how much of it was just talk. What would people have done, I wondered. Snubbed him on the street? Thrown eggs at his house?

As if reading my mind, Agnes looked up at me with a stiff-necked glare of defiance, her eyes dark as agates in the tissue-paper delicacy of her face.

"Some people want to forget what they did to him. Guard the past, paper over its secrets."

The strength of her voice was surprising, but the conversation had begun to take its toll now. Her words came more slowly and were starting very faintly to slur. Minnie came across the room and stood watchfully behind her chair.

"Mind me, girl. I don't care a tarnished pin for the past, and when you're old, you won't either. The past . . ."

She searched her mind for the rest of the sentence. "The past is a luxury. For the young."

Her old hands fumbled for the cigarette pack, then seemed to forget what they had been looking for. After a moment they dropped, defeated, into her lap.

"The point is living," she said slowly. It seemed a struggle now for her to get the words out. "Living, and having things the way...the way you want them."

She jerked her white head at the parlor windows, beyond which monotonous rain continued to fall on the little town. On the just, and the unjust. Then she straightened and seemed to fight the weariness that was now clearly overcoming her. Her final sentences came out in a hurried, slurred burst.

"I don't care about the dead. It's the living I want. They took my father away from me. They're old now, white-haired old saints."

She laughed unpleasantly, and despite her curiously muddled speech, turned a clear look of vengefulness on me.

"They're old," she repeated. "They'll die soon. I want them to die ashamed. But before that—"

Her face seemed to waver, the lucidity draining from her eyes as if a dam had broken behind them. Her head jerked sharply.

"Before that, I'll have their heads on plates. I'll grind their bones to make my bread!"

She was fading fast. Minnie stepped around and bent to her, but Agnes droned on. It was painful to watch.

"Oh, yes," she said. Her voice wavered into sly amusement. "Down the rabbit hole. In the boneyard." She tipped the dregs of her teacup into her lap and chuckled madly. "And only I am left to tell, and I will and I won't and I will and I won't."

She swiveled her head owlishly sideways. "Minnie knows. She's the one. But I fooled her, didn't I? She's an old fool, too." She cackled spitefully, seeming to enjoy my discomfort.

Beside the chair, Minnie raised her eyebrows and regretfully shook her head.

"Go away, girl," Agnes said to me. "You're too bossy. I gave you the books. What more do you want? Come back another day. Maybe I'll tell you something more—or maybe I'll be dead!"

The interview was over, if I'd really had one in the first place. Now she didn't even recognize me; she thought I was Rena. But—books?

At Minnie's urging look, I stood. "No, Agnes," I said. "You didn't give me any books. I'm Charlotte, remember? Maybe you gave books to Rena Blount?"

Agnes nodded ponderously. "Diaries," she said.

The idea was maddening. Ledgers, records—anything in Stanley Hardwicke's own hand could be invaluable to me. But diaries—for an instant I thought Rena was lucky to be dead. If she had been alive I would have throttled her myself.

Agnes slumped forward, chin touching her chest, and jerked up again.

"Peas and honey," she yelled. "Peas and honey, pudding and pie!" Her head lolled sideways and she raised it with an effort. "I *told* her and *told* her, I *already took*—"

"I think that will have to be enough," Minnie said firmly. "You can see how she is. It's only just lately, but once she started to fail—"

She held out her hands in a gesture of helpless resignation.

"It happens to all of us," she said.

In the chair, Agnes snored, then jerked awake and began to shout.

Minnie ushered me toward the door. In my hand I still held Rena's notebook. Behind us, Agnes raved, cackling and weeping.

"Minnie," I said, standing outside on the porch, "was it true? About people thinking he killed his wives, gossiping about him, or—or his getting crazy at the end? Was any of it true?"

Minnie shook her head. "I'm sorry," she said. "I know it's important to you, dear. But Agnes lives in a dream world now, most of the time. You saw how she was about her pills. I thought she might be brighter for you—she often is, in the mornings. But what she told you . . . well."

She sighed. "Leonora did kill herself, that much is true. She always was odd, and then when she learned that she was pregnant it unsettled her completely. Afterward, there was that awful rhyme the children sang for a while—I'm sure you've heard of it. As for the rest—"

She looked straight at me. "I suppose you'll find this out anyway. Stanley Hardwicke didn't just die. He wandered off somewhere, and no one ever found him. After a while, we thought he'd probably drowned. Fallen off the rocks, or jumped. There was talk then, too, but it passed. That's all there was to it."

She turned to go into the house, then looked back. "And as far as Mrs. Blount and that business about some books or other—don't take that too seriously, either, dear, will you? As far as I know, the doctor never even kept a diary."

SIX

I'D STARTED THE day believing Liane was right: Joey had seen something frightening and was hiding. But now things were different, and I thought considerably worse might have happened. He had gotten willingly into a car with a well-known young tough named Ken Biewald; only afterward had he vanished.

Rena's death looked different to me, too: less a matter of chance, and more of motive. Since the Deadly Drifter was already in jail, someone else must have done it; someone with a reason, maybe.

And then there was the notebook.

I didn't like at all what I thought about the notebook.

After all, someone had broken into Rena's house, and a little reflection made youthful prankishness an implausible explanation. Kids don't play pranks at four in the morning—not Pelican Rock kids, anyway. In fact, they don't break into murder scenes at any hour. Kids out here just hadn't gotten that bold or callous yet. As Harold Flanders said, this wasn't the city.

He'd also said nothing was missing from Rena's, and that made me wonder: why break into the house at all, if you weren't going to take anything?

Unless it wasn't there, because someone else already had it.

Someone like me, for example.

Which was ridiculous, I told myself, driving away from the Dietrich house; ridiculous and farfetched. And unnerving.

Because I did have the notebook now, and it was full of Hardwicke stuff. Only the three women's names and the chemical formula were unfamiliar to me; the rest of the lined pages were full of material I could have written myself.

In fact, I had written much of it myself: my own research, in my own green notebook. But I hadn't advertised that I was doing it, and Rena had. A dozen people heard her bragging at the workshop. A few hours later, most likely half the town knew.

It was winter, after all. The Pelican Rock gossip mill would grind anything, in winter. And a little while after she began feeding it, Rena was dead.

Ridiculous, I told myself again. No one would break into a house for a book of Hardwicke notes, much less kill for one. That was just unreasonable.

On the other hand, what someone had done to Rena was pretty unreasonable too, wasn't it?

Where is it written, after all, that killers have *good* reasons?

Unhappily thinking these things, I pulled up to the pay phone outside Mendillo's General Store and called the Dolan house.

"You're lucky Fred didn't answer," Liane said. "I mean, I'm lucky he didn't. I don't think he'd do anything to you. Did you find Joey?"

"No," I said. "But I think I've got a line on him. You mean, Fred would do something to you?"

Liane's silence answered my question. I'd suspected Fred Dolan was the type who slapped his womenfolk around, so I wasn't surprised, but the thought made me angry and more determined to try to help Liane.

"Listen," I said, "do you know a kid named Kenny Biewald?"

Her breath came out in a nervous puff. "He's no kid. And I don't want to know him."

"But you know who he is, you could point him out to me?"

"I guess so," she answered. "Why? Is Joey with him?" Her voice rose in sudden hope. It hurt to have to dash it.

She listened while I told her about my talk with Pelican Rock's Junior Underachievers. "So," I finished, "I want to ask Biewald about it."

"Oh, God," she said. I hadn't dashed as much of her hope as I'd meant to; suddenly I wondered if my efforts were simply cruel. Probably I wasn't going to find her brother. Maybe no one would; maybe it would be better to try and help her get used to that.

"Someone saw him," she said. "That's good, isn't it? I mean, he didn't just vanish into thin air, we know which way he went."

I sighed. "Sure, Liane. But what I want to know is, will you go to Fort Bragg with me? I don't want to spend all night looking, so I need someone to show me where Biewald's likely to be, and point him out to me."

Her laugh was weak but reassuring; she was a tough kid, and she wasn't coming unglued. With Fred Dolan around, that in itself was quite an accomplishment.

"I don't think you'd have any trouble finding that guy," she said. "Just look for a fist-fight, and he'd be in it. But sure, you bet I'll come. When?"

I raced through my morning chores, and shortly after noon I was outside her house, just down the lane where Fred wouldn't see me.

"I don't understand," she said when she got in the car, "what Ken Biewald would want with my brother. Or"—her brow furrowed—"maybe I do."

"Yeah," I said. "I think you might." Backing the Volkswagen between the trees, down the narrow lane to the road, I told her what I'd learned about Fred and his long romance with illegal drugs. She nodded tiredly, listening, massaging her forehead with thin fingers.

"Funny Freddy strikes again," she said when I had finished.

I pulled onto Highway One and began urging the Volkswagen up to minimum cruising velocity. Forty-five miles an hour wasn't going to break any records, but at least the speeding tractor-trailers would see us in time to swerve around us.

"Uh-huh," I said. "What more do you know about it?"

Liane bit her thumbnail. "He's always got something going," she said. "You'd think he'd know better, but I know he's dealing pot at least. I mean, for someone else it might not be such a big deal, but if he got caught again he would definitely go back to jail. They told him so when they let him out."

"He's on parole?"

She nodded. "He reports to some guy in Fort Bragg, and from what Fred says, the guy already doesn't like him. Of course, from what Fred says, nobody likes him."

I thought privately that Fred was probably right. No wonder he'd been so nervous. A parolee within sniffing distance of a murder investigation had a right to be nervous. I shifted into second gear; the Volkswagen lurched, backfired, and strained forward.

"There were some guys up here last week," she added, "from the city. Fred's got some scheme going with them, I think, but I don't know what it is. I stay out of the way when his friends are around."

I glanced over at her. She'd changed from yesterday's romantic-heroine outfit into slim jeans, a bulky gray sweater, a green fringed scarf, and narrow leather boots. She looked young, and innocent, and absolutely ravishing, and I thought she was wise to stay away from Fred's friends, because probably they weren't smart enough to stay away from her.

I was old-fashioned enough to think that seventeen-year-old girls were off-limits to friendly guys Fred Dolan's age. Of course, I hadn't thought so when I was seventeen, but that was how I'd learned to think so now. I shifted the noble Volkswagen into third gear, and asked another question.

"Were the town kids right? Did Joey know anything about Fred's dealing? Could he have gotten pot for Kenny Biewald, for instance?"

Liane shook her head, her reddish curls catching the sun as it peeped through the clouds on the horizon.

"If Fred's involved in it, Joey doesn't want to know anything about it," she said firmly. "Besides, he's not that dumb," Liane said. "Those kids don't like him, they're just awful to him. He'd know they were just using him."

That let out the idea of Fred's illegal buddies getting Joey out of the way for something he'd seen or heard around Fred. At least, it did if Fred's buddies were sensible.

On the other hand, I didn't know how big Fred's dealings were. If they were really big, then the idea wasn't let out at all, since people with large amounts of drugs, money, and guns tend not to be sensible.

For the moment, all I could do was hope Fred was as small-time as he deserved to be. Meanwhile, I had two other points to check on: Rena Blount's notebook, and Joey's impromptu car ride.

"Kenny Biewald hangs out over there," Liane said, pointing.

There was only one teenage hangout in Fort Bragg, which was a lumber town in a building slump and not well furnished with amusement for people of any age. I looked at the flashing green-and-yellow neon sign— *Steverino's Games!Games!Games!*—and decided to visit the public library first, as I had a little something I wanted to look up.

Liane apparently found the peeling facade of the library as off-putting as I found *Steverinos!* and said that she would prefer to wait in the car.

"LET'S SEE," the librarian said, running his nibbled fingertip down the column of letters and numbers in the big book open on the desk.

The Fort Bragg Public Library was not a haven for scholarly labor; neither did it offer much in the way of literary entertainment. What it most resembled, actually, was a chamber within which the long-term effects of weather might be studied.

Plastic buckets stood about on the scuffed tile floor, and the drip, drip, drip of leaks from the stained ceiling resounded hollowly in the barnlike room. A chill wind gusted over the windowsills, whose frames all seemed to recoil from their split, peeling sashes. The front door had swollen and shrunk with so many sodden winters and hot, arid summers that its latch no longer saw eye-to-eye with the strike plate; the door itself would not close properly and kept drifting open, then banging shut with every breeze, of which there were many.

The books themselves suffered from almost as serious a state of ill repair, the city fathers apparently feeling that, since they could not keep the old volumes from getting drenched, there was little point in buying any new ones. The stock, in fact, consisted mostly of outdated reference books and old farm bulletins.

An outdated reference book, however, was fine for my purposes. "Here it is," the librarian said. "C-seventeen, H-twenty-one, O-four-N-H-C-L. Cocaine Hydrochloride."

I stared at him.

"Coke," he amplified. "Snort, blow, flake, crystal, nose candy. Rich white trash."

He was at least six feet tall, unless he was standing on a box behind the desk, and he must have weighed well over one hundred and thirty pounds sopping wet, which he rarely was, to judge by the odor that hung in the damp air around him. His black oily hair looked lacquered on, and his complexion, appropriately, was the color of library paste.

"Anything else?" he asked, with a coy little hitch of his shoulders. It made me think of a snake, shedding its skin.

"No, thanks," I said, eager to be away from this unctuous fellow who seemed to be trying to make me, in his inimitable way. Librarians aren't what they were when I was a kid.

"Harlequins?" he said, waggling his eyebrows. "Sci-fi? Mysteries?" He gestured invitingly at the rack of coverless paperbacks which he kept, apparently as a lure, behind the desk.

"Do you have anything by Charlotte Kent?"

He made a face as if I'd asked for a book of Dutch kiddy-porn. "God, some lady how-to writer, isn't she? I don't have any of her."

"You won't be getting any, either," I advised him sweetly, and went on out.

Cocaine. I could believe that, like Fred Dolan, Rena might have been quietly dealing; she certainly didn't live on alimony alone. But even if she were selling drugs, why bother writing down the chemical formula? She certainly wasn't manufacturing drugs, or refining them by some complicated process.

Maybe, I thought, it wasn't Rena; maybe there really was some Hardwicke connection, after all. A little something for the bored, lonely ladies in the big houses, while the logging barons and sea captains were out in the woods, or out to sea? Something to enliven the time, when the fabric of the shining hour began to fray under the improvement of more needlework than it could stand?

But this theory, too, was fatally flawed, as I discovered when I went reluctantly back into the library to check on it. Hurrying past the Uriah Heep of the Reference Desk, I strode on through to the sparsely populated history shelves.

What I'd thought I remembered was true: the first controlled-substance laws hadn't been passed until 1914. The females of Pelican Rock might have dosed themselves dizzy, but there had been nothing illegal

about it, nor anything illegal about Doctor Hardwicke's supplying them, if he had.

Of course, it might have been a secret from the
menfolk, but all those people were dead now, and
presumably no longer kept secrets from one another.
Probably they'd all had a hearty laugh over their
earthly frailties, and I hardly thought their descen-
dants would go around committing murders to hide
the fact that Great-Great-Aunt Tillie was a dope fiend.

After all, who cared? Being a dope fiend was almost fashionable, nowadays, and everybody loved
picturesque ancestors.

I left the history aisle and headed for the science
section. It was, if possible, even more spottily sup-
plied than the history shelf. The more out-of-date a
volume was, the more likely that it could be found
here; for once, this situation served my purpose perfectly, and in the 1907 volume of *Materia Medica* I
discovered the information I was seeking.

Page 350 bore two entries for "Tablets-Cocaine,"
which in 1907 could be purchased in two strengths:
1⅛ grain, and 2¼ grain. Dissolved in one fluid dra-
mof water, or 3.7 milliliters, they produced a two-
percent or four-percent solution, respectively, and they
came in bottles of one hundred tablets, or tubes of
twenty-five.

I opened Rena's notebook. Beneath the formula for
cocaine she had written several more fragments. They
read: 1 & ⅛—2 & ¼ = 2%—4%. 25 or 100.

MOST LIKELY THOSE bottles of one hundred sold like
hotcakes in 1907. The tubes of twenty-five probably
went well around the holidays; they would be just the
right size to drop into the toe of a Christmas stock-

ing, for example, along with the orange and the walnuts and candy canes.

Fa la la, I thought, closing both books.

"Has anyone else been in to ask you about that formula recently?"

The reference librarian eyed me coyly, as if deciding what this information should cost.

"Yep. Lady. Little, cute. Not as good-looking as you, of course."

"Mm-hmm. When was that?"

He made a show of thinking about it, laying a finger against his lantern jaw. "Oh, last week, sometime. Thursday. Yep, it was Thursday, because I was packing up to leave and she came in like a house afire. All excited, like she was hot on the trail of something, and I was anxious to get out. I had a rehearsal."

He looked expectantly at me.

"I'm a rock star," he explained. "Or at least I will be."

"Oh," I said.

"I know, you don't believe me. But it's true, I'm gonna make it. I'm gonna have groupies around the block."

"Right," I said. "And you looked up the formula for her."

"Sure I did. That's my job—for now, anyway. But sooner or later, I'm gonna be a star."

"Thanks," I said, heading for the door, wishing I had a nickel for everybody in the world who hated his job and was going to be a star.

"Hey, wait—I haven't told you the name of the band."

"Surprise me," I called back.

THE NEON SIGN in the window of Steverino's
Games!Games!Games! flashed its bilious shades of
yellow and green; inside, the sounds of zapping,
buzzing, jangling video games seemed to make the
little building jump on its unsteady foundations.

An extremely large teen-age girl in a flowered smock
sat behind a counter, eating candy and dispensing
change to young men. Across from each other, she
and Liane looked like two sides of a fun-house mirror.

"I just need to talk to him for a second," I shouted,
over the din of space invaders being vaporized.

The girl's jaw went slowly around and around as she
considered this. Before she could get the wad of candy
out of her speaking apparatus, Liane pointed.

"He's over there." She stalked toward the pinball
machines; I followed.

The players here were older than the teen-age boys
fighting off the aliens at the other terminals. One of
them, tall and darkly tanned with the muscles of a
weight lifter, wore a sleeveless leather vest, leather
pants, and a Harley-Davidson eagle tattoo on his
shoulder.

Liane jerked her head at him. I wasn't surprised to
learn that this was Ken Biewald, but I was surprised to
see Marjorie Wickstrom beside him, gazing adoringly
into his face.

Her chin jutting determinedly, Liane reached out
and tapped Biewald on his tattoo.

"My brother." Her voice cut through the noise.
"What did you do with him?"

Marjorie's eyes widened, noting possible competition. Then she recognized me. Her dark hair was swept
back into a French twist; her face was made up,

heavily but carefully, accentuating her large brown eyes, delicate cheekbones, and full lips. Without her glasses she looked much older, remarkably pretty, and fragile enough to be broken in half by the young hulk looming beside her. Probably, I thought, that was part of the attraction.

Well, at least her English teacher was off the hook.

Biewald turned, eyed Liane up and down, pulled a cigarette from his vest pocket, and lit it. His eyes were strikingly blue and his face would have been handsome except for the spoiled, surly expression, the resentful curl apparently built into his lip.

"So who are you? And who's your brother?" He fed quarters into the pinball machine, grinning sideways at Liane.

I moved alongside the machine into his line of sight, ignoring Marjorie, which was just what she wanted me to do. I got the feeling she wouldn't have minded if I forgot I'd even seen her. Probably a trip to Steverino's with Ken Biewald was not her mother's idea of a nice after-school date.

"She's Joey Dolan's sister," I said to Biewald. "Joey's missing, and his mother and father want him back. And so does she. We heard you gave him a ride somewhere."

Biewald shrugged. "No skin off my ass. Stick around, though, chicky," he added to Liane. "You're pretty cute. Maybe later we c'n go somewhere, talk about it."

Once more his gaze traveled up one side of her and down the other. Then, slowly, lasciviously, he winked.

Liane's response was a single bored twitch of her eyebrow.

Smiling as if to say he thought she would change her mind later, Biewald pulled the knob on the right side of the pinball machine and began to work the levers. Lights flashed, bells rang, and the points began at once to jangle up onto the display.

Marjorie sulked.

"The police are looking for him," I shouted.

The players on either side of me looked up, their faces frozen in cautious hostility. Biewald kept pummeling the levers.

"If I don't find him, they'll be asking. You drove him up here from Pelican Rock, didn't you? Yesterday? Where did you leave him?" Already I was getting hoarse.

Biewald dropped his cigarette and stepped on it.

"Lady, get the hell out of here."

Briskly, Liane brushed past me, stepped to the back of the machine, reached behind it, and yanked the plug. The display went dark; the bells fell silent. Marjorie's mouth dropped open.

Biewald's stare was a mixture of fury and astonishment; clearly, he didn't think the chicky was cute any more.

He took a step.

"Right," Liane said, thin fists clenched at her sides. "Beat me up. That'll fix everything, won't it?"

She sniffed in disdain. "Go ahead. It won't be the first time. Tough guy," she spat at him. "Only when you're done, I'll rip your lungs out if you don't tell me where my brother is."

It occurred to me that Fred Dolan had not been an entirely useless influence on her. Can't spoil good material, I thought admiringly.

Still, Biewald was big. And mean.

The other players were staring now, waiting to see what he would do. I stiffened my spine, straightened my shoulders, stuck out my chin, and tried not to think about how completely, utterly terrified I was.

The fat girl at the counter had her hand on the telephone, ready to call the cops or an ambulance. Biewald just stood staring, apparently trying to decide if Liane was crazy, which was what I was trying to decide, too. I decided *I* was.

Suddenly, he was laughing. He leaned on the pinball machine and shook, pointing at Liane with one grease-blackened finger. Around him, the others laughed too, in relief, and went back to their games.

The girl at the counter put down the phone and began to open another candy bar. Beside me, Marjorie managed a weak smile.

"You...you...," Biewald gasped. "You are one dumb little broad, you know that?"

She took a deep breath. "Yeah. But I really need to find my brother." And that was her mistake; at once his interest began waning. Just because she'd gotten his attention didn't mean she'd be able to reason with him.

I stepped in. "Listen, we're just trying to save you some trouble." This was a lie, but under the circumstances I thought an eminently justifiable one; we weren't safely out of here yet. "You had to let him out of the car. We just want to know where, that's all."

He chuckled again, pushing past me to plug in the pinball machine again. It lit up "tilt," and he smacked the side of it with his open hand, then fed in two more quarters.

"I dumped him by the beach road just above town, the dumb little bastard. He was no use to me. What'd he do, rob somebody's piggy bank?"

I shook my head. "The police want to question him about a murder."

Biewald blinked, a blank look sliding easily onto his face. "Murder? Hey, who'd he murder?"

"Nobody. Thanks. That's all we needed." I turned to go, passing hurriedly between the game consoles, calculating the distance between Steverino's and the safety of my car with Liane stepping fast right alongside me.

When we got to the main drag, I looked back, but no one was following, or at least I could not see anyone. A few more steps brought us to the car; I smiled at Liane and with great relief reached out to unlock the passenger door.

A hard brown hand reached from behind me and grabbed my wrist hard, and spun me around. Ken Biewald stood there.

Marjorie wasn't with him, and he wasn't smiling.

"You don't have to tell no cops about me and that kid. They'd love to get me on something like murder." His fierce look went speculative. "When was it, anyway? I been, uh, out of it. Partyin' with Margie, you know."

I didn't know, but no doubt Marjorie would write a poem about it, and I would find out.

"Yesterday afternoon," Liane answered him. "Around the time you let my brother out of your car."

If you did, I thought.

"That's all right, then," he said. "I'm covered for that. At least, I will be if you find that kid." He stepped toward Liane, grinning in the evident belief that a silver front tooth had some sort of allure.

I reached in front of him to unlock Liane's door; she got in hastily.

"I been at my brother's house, way up in Westport," Biewald went on. "I'm covered in the Rock—people saw me there. An' I'm covered up here 'cause everybody in Steverino's knows I was shootin' pool 'fore I went to my brother's. But between here an' there, I got a problem, don't I, until that kid shows up? Stupid little bastard, he was, an' now it turns out he's my alibi!"

WE DROVE BACK south on Highway One in silence.

I believed Ken Biewald. If he'd killed Rena, I doubted he would have put himself anywhere near the beach road at the time of her murder. He'd have said he dropped Joey off somewhere else.

Which put Joey near Rena's when she died. Maybe Liane had been right; maybe Joey had seen something frightening. Worse, I thought someone frightening may have also seen him.

And taken him, perhaps, along with the gun. And that brought me back to *why*?

Rena had been killed for a reason. When I learned that reason, I could find out whose it was.

And that person would tell me where to find Joey, because I would throttle that person with my hands until that person did.

Liane wanted to be dropped off to stay the night with friends at a commune halfway between Fort Bragg and Pelican Rock. With some misgivings, I pulled down the long cedar-lined driveway that led to the main house there. But my suspicions about possibly dope-addled residents were quashed almost immediately; the place contradicted every idea I'd had about what a commune would be like.

The garden that ran along the drive looked as if no weed would ever dare rear its head among the mulched, deep-green rows of carrots and lettuce; the dirt paths connecting the small outbuildings were neatly swept and edged with stones. As we neared the house, a big yellow retriever got up from his mat on the porch, stretched, and wagged his tail expectantly.

Inside, by the kitchen wood-stove, a gray cat sat on a braided rug, lapping at a blue bowl full of milk. The house smelled of cinnamon and oranges. A thin young man sat at the kitchen table, mending socks; he stood as I came in, and offered me a chair.

I said no, regretfully; the rocker by the stove looked comfortable, and the spotless room was peaceful and warm.

Liane had taken off her jacket and was crouched beside the cat, stroking it; as I turned to go she looked up and smiled a little sadly.

"I guess we didn't get far with Kenny Biewald, did we?"

"We know more than we did," I told her. I didn't tell her that what we knew made me very anxious; it wouldn't have done any good.

And as for myself, all I wanted was to go home; with any luck I could make my own kitchen feel as safe and cozy as this one. A little reluctantly, I left Liane in her haven and drove away, looking forward to a quiet evening and a hot toddy.

But it was not to be. The car began to sputter as I pulled off the highway, and died as I rolled into Pelican Rock. I let it coast to the side of the road and got out, cursing.

Raising the hood turned out to be pointless; dark liquid flowed in a steady stream out of the crankcase, over the gravel and into the ditch. I looked at my watch: five-fifteen, and already pitch-dark. Milton's garage was closed by now, and at this hour a tow truck from Fort Bragg would cost fifty dollars.

Nervously, I regarded the dark road.

Then, heck, I thought. If anyone did want to harm me, they'd hardly expect to find me walking two miles home in the rainy night.

Nothing stirred as I crossed the highway. The drifting mist smelled of salt and eucalyptus. Away off the cliffs, fog buoys honked. Stray winds sent showers of droplets down from the trees looming close on either side of the road.

I stayed off the gravel shoulder, striding soundlessly down the middle of the pavement and congratulating myself on my decision. The walk was pleasantly refreshing, and I'd gotten almost a quarter of a mile up Little Lake Road when I heard the car approaching from behind.

Its headlights cast wide shiny patches on the wet blacktop. Its engine slowed as it neared and the driver caught sight of me.

Quickly I stepped to the side of the road, to let it go by.

Instead, it slid alongside. Then it stopped.

"CHARLOTTE, WHAT THE hell are you doing wandering around alone?"

It was Harold Flanders, in the Dodge. He leaned out the window, looking exasperated.

"Car broke down. I'm walking. Is that against the law?"

He waved me around to the passenger side.

"Get in here. I'll drive you home. You think you're indestructible, Charlotte? You think nothing bad could happen to you, is that what you think?"

I got into the car. "I should ask you what you're doing. I didn't know you ran a twenty-four-hour travelers' aid."

He shrugged in disgust, and gunned the engine. "I'm driving around, thinking. Bremer's been handing me lots of grief. Good thing I gave you a good character reference, that's all I've got to say to you."

"I guess he wants to arrest somebody, huh?" I tried not to sound uneasy, but Rena's notebook seemed to be radiating its presence from my bag. I didn't want to know what Sheriff Bremer would make of that.

Harold nodded. "Geez, but he's an idiot." He paused. "You look like ten days of rain, yourself. Who's giving you grief? Peter?"

I glanced at him in surprise. Harold was only about ten years older than I was, in his mid-forties, but I thought of him as more settled. He was married, and he had a couple of kids and a house at the ocean end of town, in the little section called Portugee Flats. He kept a vegetable garden in the back, and when he wasn't working, he was tending it, or playing catch with his little boy. Sometimes he barbecued out there; I'd seen him turning hamburgers, wearing a chef's hat and a bibbed apron that said Give The Cook A Drink in big red letters.

I'd thought his life looked boring, routine, and that he had looked ridiculous in the apron and hat. None of it seemed ridiculous now, though: a house, a family, things he could count on. Things he knew wouldn't vanish, or dissolve. I envied the way he'd gotten the hang of the barbecue outfit.

I bit my lip. "Peter?" I said. "No, not really."

He was going to cause me grief, though. Suddenly I realized I hadn't thought much about Peter lately and hadn't wanted to. The chemistry was still there, but that was all.

Peter, I knew, would not be caught dead in a chef's hat, or any of the rest of it.

By the light of the dashboard I saw the sympathy in Harold's eyes and realized that he understood. The road curved and climbed sharply upward under the redwoods. It was very dark, and the dashboard lights glowed cozily like little beacons.

"I heard you two were an item," he went on. "Didn't expect it would last, if you'll pardon my saying so."

I turned, wanting, I suppose, an excuse. "You didn't? Why?"

"Oh, I don't know. Just doesn't seem your type. Flighty, or something." He glanced at me, and smiled. "Tell you the truth, before you took up with him, I kind of had you picked out for a fellow I know, up to Fort Bragg."

I had to laugh, wondering what sort of fellow Harold would pick out for me.

"He's a quiet sort. Kind of stubborn, goes his own way." Harold chuckled. "Independent as a hog on ice, is what he is, actually. I figured you two would probably hit it off pretty good. But then you got busy."

He turned into Everts Lane. The lights of my house showed faintly through the redwoods. "I mean," he went on, "I'm sorry your heart's getting busted, if it is. But if you're going to split up with old Peter, well, I can't say I'm sorry about that."

"You don't like him, do you?" It wasn't really a question. Harold always treated Peter with distant courtesy, nothing more.

His eyebrows went up consideringly. "Wouldn't say that. Wouldn't say so at all. Just never quite got a grip on him, but there's nothing wrong with that. Lots of fellows I don't understand. You want to meet this friend of mine, though, I can arrange it. Little get-together at my place next Saturday, in fact. What do you say?"

I shook my head. "It's good of you, Harold. But really, I don't think I can. I've got too many things on my mind, and too much to do. If things straighten out by Saturday, I'm just going to catch up on my sleep."

He pulled the Dodge up in the patch of gravel in front of the cottage and put it in neutral. "Mmm," he said. "Too bad. My buddy Solli'll be disappointed. Don't suppose your being so busy has anything to do with the Dolan boy?"

He didn't wait for me to answer. "I wondered," he said, "if you happened on anything."

I hesitated. He wasn't asking an idle question, I knew. In addition to his other qualities, Harold was sharp as a cat's whisker. It was how he'd known about me ending it with Peter, before I'd really known about it myself.

"'Cause if you have," he went on, "it would help me a lot to hear about it. That Bremer, he's making my life a misery. Wants another term in the worst way, you know, and he thinks riding my tail is the way to get it."

He looked at me, his face expectant in the faint glow from the dashboard.

"By the way, I meant to tell you. You handled yourself real well out there. When you found her, I mean. Lots of people, come across that, they'd come right unglued. Not just women, either."

"Thanks," I said. After a moment, Harold shifted the car back into drive, and I got out.

"Well," he said, "like I told you, if you come across anything, it'd help me a lot. Sure would like to get old Sheriff Bremer out of my yard and back into his own."

His car began to roll forward.

"Harold, wait."

He stopped.

"Maybe I have found some things. I don't know. Maybe you should decide. Do you want to come in?"

Harold grinned, turning off the ignition.

I brought him in, sat him down, and fixed us both drinks while Ninki twined about our feet, making welcoming noises. We settled at the kitchen table, where the cups and ashtrays from the search for Joey that seemed so long ago still stood messily.

I didn't know where to begin, so for a start I took Rena's notebook from my bag and laid it on the table. Then I opened my mouth, but I was so tired, the words that came out weren't even mine; I could only repeat a favorite line, from an old *Bert and I* record. It wasn't original, but it seemed awfully appropriate.

"Harold," I said, "my day has been just one long fizzle, from beginning to end."

"Oh," he said when I had finished. "*Oh*, how I would like to arrest your silly carcass and toss it in jail for sheer damn clumsiness. Charlotte. Why did you have to pick up that notebook?"

"I didn't know I was picking it up," I said humbly. I'd already told him this, but I thought the point worth repeating.

Harold looked unmollified. "Do you know what Bremer is going to say when I tell him you were in competition with her, and now you've got her notes?"

He gave me a dark glance. I guess he didn't think killers had to have good reasons, either.

"And Joey Dolan," he went on, "—*you* know who picked him up and who saw him last. You know all this stuff. Why you? That's what Bremer's going to say."

"Yes," I said. "But—you wouldn't have to tell him how you came by all this information, would you? Except for the notebook, I mean. Because since I didn't do it, and someone else did, the investigation is going to aim at someone else anyway, sooner or later. Isn't it?"

Harold frowned.

"And," I went on, "*with* all this new information, that could happen pretty soon. Couldn't it?"

Harold frowned harder. "It's not much, Charlotte. It's not even all that helpful. It's just the kind of stuff that makes you look so—involved. Besides," he finished unhappily, "I have to tell him."

My turn to frown.

"I have to tell him," Harold said, "just as soon as he gets back from the California State Law Enforcement Convention."

I blinked at him. "You mean—"

"He left this morning," Harold said, "right after he got finished jumping all over me. Three days, though, and he'll be back from drooling over all that state-of-the-art firepower the vendors are showing there. I can see it now—he'll want lasers, stun guns, infrared..."

"And then?"

"I'll have to say that I've at least had you under surveillance. You had a beef with her, you found her, you had plenty of time to go snooping through her place, and you've got the notebook. Also, you had access to the Dolan boy's shotgun. I suppose you do know how to load and fire it?"

"Uh-huh," I said. I wasn't much with lasers or stun guns, but I'd been only eight the first time a twelve-gauge kick knocked me on my blue-jeaned bottom. After that I'd learned fast; my dad wanted a son, but when he got me instead, he made the best of it.

Harold headed for the door, Rena's notebook in hand.

"You don't think I did kill her, though, do you, Harold?"

He turned, tiredly rubbing his forehead. "Oh, hell, no." His voice was friendly again, though much put-upon. "Your story's too damn silly, and besides— well, I just don't, that's all," he finished stubbornly. "Man's gotta trust something, and what I trust is what my insides tell me."

He sighed. "But that doesn't mean I'll be able to convince Bremer, unless I give him somebody who looks better for it than you. You should wish me luck, is all I've got to say."

Which I did, forcefully and sincerely. But as I watched the Dodge's tail lights disappear into darkness, I didn't feel any luck gathering around me, or around Harold, either.

Not good luck, anyway.

Meeyeeowwrowll, said Ninki. *Mrrowwyee-owlmrrowwll.*

"Yeah," I said, turning away from the dark window. "Yeah, my sentiments exactly."

SEVEN

HILLSIDE CEMETERY WAS bounded on three sides by whitewashed pickets, and on the fourth by a seven-foot Cyclone fence that the highway department had erected. The highway lay just beyond the steeply sloping meadow, which was studded with white granite markers; whether the bureaucrats thought cars would invade the plots and vandalize the tombstones, or whether they thought the dead might illegally cross over Highway One come Judgment Day, no one could tell.

For whatever reason, the strands of barbed wire at the top of the metal fence sections gave the far end of the graveyard an air of institutional dreariness. Beyond the chain-links, trucks roared by with tedious regularity, shattering the peace that passeth all understanding, and leaving a stink.

It was in this section that Rena's grave had been dug. Now she was about to be lowered into it, in a coffin whose inside panels were blue quilted silk. She had not been viewed, as the horrid phrase went, for obvious reasons, but the blue silk had been advertised by local rumor. In this case, rumor was probably accurate.

Pelican Rock took care of its own pretty well. Rena hadn't been quite the town's own, having some years before been married to, and then divorced from, a businessman who'd built a vacation house here. When she was alive the townsfolk would never let her forget her non-native status; her determination to be in on everything hadn't helped. But now she was dead, no longer apt to be such a pushy pest, and they were willing to plaster over the differences with a wreath of flowers and a hole six feet deep.

Although I had not wanted to come, I knew that in Pelican Rock one missed such events at one's peril; ever afterward, if I did not appear, I would be someone who did not show up for Rena's funeral.

I tried to imagine her peacefully at rest on the bed of quilted blue, but the effort ended badly. It seemed to me that she must be screeching protest even now, thumping the padded silk with her fists and clawing the watertight seals of the box that enclosed her.

I clenched my own fists tightly together and pressed my knuckles hard up under my chin, and held myself still. We were just the same age, Rena and I, and now she was dead, and I knew well enough that the watertight seals wouldn't hold very long.

Mist beaded on the blooms of the salmon-colored funeral gladiolas splayed over the coffin. At the other side of the grave, Harold Flanders stood, looking grim and wearing a tan trenchcoat, a navy suit, and black wing-tip shoes.

Symbolic dirt fell into the glads and clattered on the veneer of the coffin. The minister said some meaningless words. Then it was over.

The others were leaving: the minister, Aaron Williams, Jean Weston, Martin McGregor who would probably write up the funeral for his column, and a skimpy contingent from the local chapter of the Order of the Eastern Star. Minnie Taylor was there, too, wearing a powder-blue raincoat and a navy straw hat with a pink silk rose on it, looking as if someone ought to be photographing her for *Vogue*.

I looked down the hill toward the cluster of houses and stores; from where I stood, I could see almost straight into Agnes Dietrich's kitchen windows. It must be strange, I thought, to look out every morning into a graveyard. Unsettling to see, every day of your life, the hillside where you would spend the days after your death; unsettling, or comforting, depending on your point of view.

Of course, Agnes wouldn't wind up on this side of the hill. She would lie in the family plot, whose marble monuments stood almost in her backyard. I began to walk down toward that section, which was divided off from the rest of the cemetery by a low wrought-iron scrollwork fence.

Harold Flanders walked beside me, having agreed to transport me to and from the service. We left by the back gate, crossed the road, and got into his car.

He sighed. "You know, Charlotte, I should have been a fireman, like my dad. Lots simpler—you find a fire, you put it out. That's all."

"Something's happened?" We pulled away from the graveyard, toward the highway.

"What's happened is I arrested Elmer Wainwright for drunk and disorderly, last night. Seems he got loaded and started breaking up the Sea Gull when the guys there wouldn't believe the story he was telling them."

"The story," I said, knowing even then what kind of thing must be coming. After all, Elmer had told me where he got his stories.

Harold nodded. "Seems Elmer's mother told him Rena Blount was strangled. Strangled by the neck, as he put it. And Elmer maintains as how she ought to know, he said, seeing as she speaks to him from the grave."

"So I've heard," I said. "Poor Elmer."

"Yeah," Harold said severely. "There's only one thing, though, about poor Elmer and his story."

I looked at him. "You don't mean—"

He nodded. "Yep. She was. Autopsy report came back late last evening. Manual fracture of the larynx and trachea was the cause of death. Shotgun came later."

"Harold, do you think Elmer might have been in on it somehow? Or did it?"

He shook his head. "Not the strangling part, anyway. Killer was right-handed. Elmer's a lefty. And to my mind, the Dolan kid's really ruled out now, too. It takes nerve to strangle somebody, and from what you say, the kid didn't have that."

He sighed. "No, as far as Elmer goes, I think he just got drunk and talkative. You know Elmer—he's about as deadly as a pan of warm milk."

"But . . . how did Elmer know?"

Harold glanced at me and shrugged. "I don't know, Charlotte, I just don't know anything about this, and between you and me I'm having a hell of a time trying to figure it. You mind a little cruise? My mother used to say it blows the stink off."

Considering the event we had just left, I thought we could use something like that; Harold turned onto Highway One, headed north, and after a few miles turned left onto Albion Road, along the bluffs. After a little while the reason for the drive became clearer to me; Harold wanted someone to bounce his ideas off, someone who would not, like Sheriff Bremer, throw them back in his face.

I felt quite flattered that he had picked me; one way and another, I was beginning to appreciate him more and more, and I thought if the fellow he'd picked out for me in Fort Bragg was anything like him, I'd give it a go. In the future, of course. Sometime when I wasn't so tired, and busy.

And if I wasn't in jail.

"Okay," Harold said, holding up a blunt, brown index finger. "We know Rena headed home about noon or so. At least that's the last time anybody admits to seeing her. So let's say she drove straight home. She's inside, with all the doors and windows locked, by one or one-ten. We found everything except the front door closed up tight as a drum, and nothing was forced. Which means—"

"The killer was someone she knew, someone she trusted and let in."

A hundred yards from the edge of the road, whitecaps surged on a leaden sea. No horizon line broke the dreary sweep of dark gray waves and streaming sky, the one blending sullenly into the other far out at some cold, unmarkable spot. The gulls were white smears on a dark palette, wheeling and crying among the rocks.

Harold pulled the car to the side of the road and turned off the engine. Below, breakers crashed against the huge pillars of rock with a steady roar, sending up gouts and foamy white fountains of spray.

"Maybe she was even glad to see him," he said. "Maybe she was afraid, and that was why she had everything locked up. But he killed her, with his hands, and then a couple of hours later she got blasted."

He pounded his clenched fists gently on the wheel.

"Maybe he didn't have a shotgun when he killed her, and later when he got it, he did what he'd wanted to do all along," I said. "Why did he want to, that's my question. In the heat of the moment I guess I can see being mad enough to mutilate someone. But I can't see hanging around for hours and then doing it."

Harold looked at me. He seemed to be listening carefully.

"Who could stay mad that long?" I went on. "I mean, it would sink in that she was dead, you'd already killed her, you'd gotten your vengeance or whatever. And why would the killer want to stay around there, anyway? To get caught?"

He nodded. "But if he didn't stay around—and we're just saying 'he' for simplicity's sake, because it could have been a woman—why come back?

"Besides," he went on, "you've left out one other thing. Joey Dolan is missing. The gun was his. It was covered with his prints, fresh and unsmudged. No one put on gloves to fire it, or anything like that, and no other prints were on it."

A little bell went off in my head. "None?"

Harold shook his head.

"Harold, I took the gun away from Joey earlier that morning. Shouldn't mine have been there?"

He frowned. "Yeah. Probably. You can thank your stars they weren't, too. Even I wouldn't be able to let that go."

"But," I said, "if Joey's fingerprints and *no one else's* are on that gun, then there is, as far as I'm concerned, only one way they could have gotten there."

Harold stared at me. "Afterward," he said softly.

"Right," I said. "Wiped, and then given to Joey to handle. Look at it this way. Somebody goes to the Dolan place looking for Joey. Maybe somebody who thinks he's been seen near Rena's when she was killed. Whoever it is finds the gun on the porch, nabs Joey, blows Rena's dead body away, and then wipes the gun and makes Joey handle it, so only his fingerprints will be on it."

Harold nodded, but he looked troubled. "It's reasonable," he said, "as far as it goes. But it's far-fetched, too. Why would anyone go to all that trouble? And assuming they did go to all that trouble, why wait hours before doing it?"

"Disguise," I told him. "You told me, didn't you, that there had been a couple of others? A series of killings?"

Harold started the car. "Yep. Real disappointing, too, when we found out that fella already got picked up, over in Willits the day before."

"Maybe our murderer was disappointed. Maybe our murderer found out too late that the Willits psycho was in custody when Rena died. So when he—or she—got Joey and the gun, it seemed like a good idea to kill two birds with one stone."

Harold frowned. "Spell it out for me again?"

"Harold, I thought you wanted me to give up the murder business."

He grinned, eyes on the road. "I do. After this one is all tied up. Come on, Sherlock, give."

That was another thing I liked about Harold. You couldn't threaten him. All he cared about was getting the job done, not where the good ideas came from. And when he found a source of them, he was not above handing out flattery to get a few more; he had pride, but no false pride.

"Someone killed Rena," I said, "hoping you'd think the psycho did it. Then, bad luck—Joey got out of Kenny Biewald's car near Rena's house. If Biewald let him out near Beach Road, it would be shorter for him to walk back to town that way, wouldn't it? So he did, and as he walked by he saw the killer leaving Rena's.

"Now," I went on, "there is an inconvenient witness. Solution—remove Joey *and* pin the murder on him by creating, in effect, a false crime, with false evidence."

We passed the Art Center and the post office, and pulled up in front of Dietrich's garage. I thought the town gossip mill would be whirring soon, grinding news of Charlotte Kent taking leisurely drives with Harold Flanders. Luckily, I am the type who thinks it is the function of some of us to amuse the rest of us; also, luckily, Harold's wife was not burdened with an overactive imagination.

"Thanks for the lift," I said, and got out.

Harold nodded absently and pulled away, looking worried, a fact that bothered me more than it might have in anyone else. When Harold looked worried, it was usually because there was something to worry about; he and his wife were alike that way. I knew what I was thinking about Joey, and it unnerved me to find that Harold was thinking it, too.

I hadn't liked even faintly suspecting that Joey had done something awful to someone. Now, though, it was getting steadily more likely that someone had done something awful to him. He was either the villain or a victim, and between those two dismal possibilities, I realized that I liked the second one a whole lot less.

You can get acquitted of murder, I thought unhappily, walking into Dietrich's garage where, to my unhappy surprise, my car's innards still lay strewn on the cement floor. But you can't get acquitted of being dead. And dead was what I was starting to be afraid Joey was.

Milton himself came into the office, wiping his hands on a greasy rag. He had the look of a surgeon who has gone in to remove a hot appendix and has found cancer.

"Miz Kent," he said, stuffing the rag in his coverall pocket, "I got good news, and I got bad news."

The good news was that it would only take a week to get the parts.

I RESIGNED MYSELF to another walk. It was as I approached Hillside Cemetery from the back side that I saw something odd: a dot of pink, bobbing against the green grass. Minnie Taylor was getting briskly up from the spot where she had been kneeling. I paused, watching her make her way among the cedars, away from the cluster of old marble headstones, down the hill.

Out of curiosity, I crossed the road and entered the cemetery by the back gate. What, I wondered, could keep Minnie kneeling on the damp grass for so long? She wasn't near Rena's grave any longer, not that I really thought Minnie would spend that much time praying for Rena. A few minutes, perhaps, but not half the morning.

I climbed the wet, grassy hillside and approached the spot where Minnie had been. It was the Hardwicke family plot, I saw with surprise, and Minnie had taken the pink silk rose from her hat and left it there, weighted with a rock, in front of the large marble monument in the shape of a leaning cross.

I looked down the hill. She was on the road now, walking quickly toward the Art Center, not looking back.

I turned back to the marker. It was a very large slab of marble, and on it were carved the Hardwicke names, all the way back to Hester and Zachariah, born in Maine, grandparents to the unlucky Stanley.

Stanley himself, of course, was not here. His body, according to Minnie, had never been found.

In fact, for such a nice cemetery, Hillside had a lot of vacancies. My curiosity spurred anew by Stanley Hardwicke's absence, I wandered among the markers until I found the plots belonging to three other families: Upson, Tate and Walsh.

No Cordelia. No Eliza. No Margaret. Perhaps, I thought, they had married and now lay with husband's kin. But I didn't think so. Rena had put them in her notebook under their maiden names. I hurried home, and called the county clerk's office.

The woman who answered was cheerful and quick.

"Here we are," she said, "Cordelia Upson, born 1901. Eliza Tate, same year, March twelfth. And Margaret Walsh, 1902, January fifth."

"What about deaths?" I asked. "I mean, I suppose they might still be alive, but they'd be pretty old, and I was wondering—"

"Looks to me like they're all three still kicking," the woman said. "'Course, they might have moved away. If they've died, at any rate, we don't know about it. Tell you what, if you find out any of them have, will you let me know? Because I don't have death dates for any one of these three, and I like to keep the records up-to-date if I can."

I agreed that of course I would. Then I asked another question. Her response was brisk and efficient, as before.

"Oh, my," she said, "Stanley Hardwicke. Been a long time since I've heard that name said around here. You the little girl I heard about, came in last year with the notebook and questions? Old Matthew was working for me when my fingers went out with the rheumatism, you'd have seen him."

I admitted that I was indeed that little girl.

A chuckle came through the telephone line. "Yes, well, Matthew's from the Rock, you know. He's not about to go shooting the breeze about Doc Hardwicke—his sister-in-law used to be a Pelican Rock girl. People there don't talk about him much—s'pose you've found that out."

The amount of good luck I'd just stumbled on made me catch my breath and wait. After a moment, I managed to make a sound that the woman on the other end apparently took as invitation to continue.

"Thing is," she said, "there is an official date of death for Stanley Hardwicke."

"An official date," I said.

"Yep. S'pose that's what Matthew gave out to you."

I said that he had.

"And I suppose," she went on, "no one in the Rock saw fit to tell you anything more?"

"Not until lately."

"'Course they wouldn't," the woman said. "I'm from Booneville, myself—always thought they were mighty strange up in the Rock, where he was concerned, anyways. Thing is, there's no real date for his death. Just a paper one, 'cause nobody saw the man pass on.

"Way I heard it," she went on, "he just vanished. Few scoops short of a pailful, the way I heard tell—in his mind, I mean. Some kind of nastiness in the story I never understood really right—'course, as I say, I wasn't much bigger'n a bug, only heard what the grown folks said. Those days, little girls didn't hear no nasty things, you know."

I thought of Liane, and the number of nasty things she'd had to hear in her young life.

"Thank you," I said. "Miz—?"

"Mrs.," she said firmly. "Mrs. Jane Kilmer. You pass by, you'll see my mailbox out to the orchard end of Booneville. Stop in if you care to—and by the way, while I've got you on the line—how's Minnie holding up?"

"Minnie Taylor?"

"The very one," my cheerful informant agreed. "My brother courted Minnie awhile, but he never could win her. We all thought she had another beau somewhere, but if she did he never did work out, as I know she never married. We did correspond for a time, and then I lost track of her, though I heard tell of her. Awful about that great-nephew of hers, isn't it?"

I said Minnie was fine, and admitted I hadn't been around town long enough to hear about any nephew, awful or otherwise.

"Guess the news hasn't gotten around yet," Mrs. Kilmer said briskly. "I just heard it from my sister, over in Ukiah—she's married to a cook in the jail there. Turns out it was Minnie's niece's boy they arrested for all them murders. Deadly Drifter, they called him, or some such nonsense. She raised him, you know, for all the thanks she ever got out of it."

Mrs. Kilmer paused long enough to draw breath. "Regular hoodlum, he was," she went on, evidently relishing the subject. "Racketing around in that car of his, made her life a misery. Take off for weeks, getting into all kinds of trouble, and then when he got caught he'd always be calling her, wanting bail money or whatever. Had a violent streak in him, too. Well, he's been gone for over a year now, and if they lock him up, I say it's a blessing, and she's well shut of him."

So, I thought when we had hung up, Minnie had told me the straight story. Stanley Hardwicke had vanished. Like Cordelia, Margaret, and Eliza.

And like Joey.

More interestingly, though, the original likeliest suspect in Rena's murder had connections in Pelican Rock. Not only family connections, I was willing to wager; guys who like racketing around generally liked racketing around with somebody.

Could somebody have known the Deadly Drifter was about to be arrested, and tried to slip one more murder onto his résumé? Gotten the timing wrong, perhaps because Minnie's nephew got picked up earlier than expected?

Connections were what I'd wanted in the first place, and now I had them. The trouble was, they didn't line up the way I'd hoped. They didn't produce answers; they only gave me more questions.

I now had questions, in fact, the way some people have hives. And not a dab of an answer to put on them.

"YOU SURE IT'S all right," Dawes said, "me comin' around so late? Not inconvenient or anything." The ghost of a gleam came into his eye as he saw my poor sink with all its parts scattered on the red formica counter.

It was five-thirty, but I would have waited until midnight to get that sink repaired; I was tired of filling the teapot from the bathtub spigot. And I'd gone cold turkey on home repair; if I did some of it, I might be tempted to write another book of it.

"Of course it's all right. Go right ahead."

Reflexively brushing his lucky rabbit's foot, he headed for his task.

I carried my notebook, and the pile of writing-workshop envelopes that I had been avoiding, into the living room. That way, while I tried to distract myself from thoughts of Joey, I could keep the corner of my eye on Dawes. But despite Rose Arguello's warning, he showed not the slightest inclination to poke or pry anywhere except into that sink's innards, and within an hour he had installed the necessary new pipes and valves and sealers, and was done.

"That'll be twenty-seven fifty," he said, and as I counted the bills he apologetically added, "It wouldn't be so much, except I had to replace some things. Give you a list of 'em, if you want."

"I'm sure what you did was just right, Dawes. I'm surprised you don't charge extra, coming out all this way."

He touched his lucky charms once again and gave the wan suggestion of a smile.

"Yuh," he said, picking up his toolbox and moving toward the door. "Sink's a delicate thing, y'know. You got to appreciate a sink. Treat it right, it'll treat you right. Abuse it"—he made a fountaining gesture with his free hand—"whammo."

I assured him that I would not do anything at all to make any plumbing in my house go whammo, and with a final ponderous nod he left the convalescent sink in my care.

I turned to the writing-workshop manuscripts. Marjorie's new poem was entitled "Flaming Surrender," and I thought it boded ill for Kenny Biewald; since abandoning the English teacher, she had learned more anatomy than a medical student, but she was not old enough for Kenny to have legally taught it to her.

It amazed me how she got those parts and their workings to rhyme so well. Lunge and plunge were obvious, of course, as were the recurrent rapture and capture, but the others suggested a heretofore unknown synthesis between biology and onomatopoeia.

Ooze and muse I thought not strictly kosher, but then I was less a student in the genre than Marjorie. The kid, I thought, probably had a great future; I only hoped it wouldn't be in the witness box.

I read on through the rest of the workshop's submissions then, grinning in spite of myself at Emily Wetmore's "Ode to a Blackened Eye," which was the cleverest takeoff on Grecian urns I had ever seen; I paged sadly through Kieran Gray's scratchings and the rest of the stuff, and thence to supper, and thence to bed, wondering all the while why the idea of plumbing bothered me so intensely.

Clearly, Dawes's advice was correct. A sink was a delicate thing. If it had major surgery, it ought not to bear any stresses or strains for a little while. And yet the idea made me uneasy.

Once, after an outdoor expedition, a wood tick burrowed into my ear, and it bothered me the same way. A something where no something ought to be— I didn't know then either, of course, what the something was—until I worried and worried it with the tip of my little finger and at last it came scrabbling awfully out.

The next morning, I had a dilly of a headache.

Also, I had the answer, or part of it. Plumbing, indeed. I thought I'd better call Harold right away.

But Harold's line was busy, and as I reached for the phone to try him yet again, it rang at me.

MINNIE TAYLOR lived only a couple of miles from me, on the small hillside farm her father had established a hundred years earlier; now, as a few thin rays of sunshine slanted weakly through high billows of fog, the old homestead seemed to shimmer in a hazy, transient glow, like a mirage of days gone by. Redwood rail fencing marched smartly along the edges of the yard and the pasture, within which a dozen shaggy goats nudged each other to nibble the choicest clumps of grass.

A gravel drive, freshly raked, led in to the closed side doors of the weathered gray barn, which, like the house, was set into the steep hillside; alongside it, whitewashed rabbit hutches stood in a neat row. Fresh yellow straw had been spread beneath them, and in the straw a few plump Rhode Island Red hens nestled amiably to catch the scarce warmth of the day.

A wisp of smoke curled from the chimney of the house, beyond which Minnie's garden spread like a horticulturist's dream, the rail-edged beds brimming full of rich black loam quite unlike the poor sandy stuff in my own yard. On raised pallets, tubs of begonia and fuchsia spilled cascades of blooms, purple and red; along the curving walkway, masses of deep-blue lobelia surrounded clots of pale green primroses getting ready to flower.

But the main show of the garden now was the poppy bed: huge orange-yellow explosions of shimmery petals, bobbing proudly on slender stems, row on row, like exquisite soldiers. The California poppy grew only in Northern California, but it was a common, unextravagant flower; Minnie had somehow found or created this varietal that bloomed early and resembled a patch of sunshine in the oncoming gloom.

One look at the place told why Minnie Taylor was so remarkably strong, energetic, and fit: unremitting hard work. The garden and yard looked as if two strong men spent a couple of hours every day maintaining it, but they didn't. Minnie did it all.

The sun vanished for good behind the gathering fog bank as I knocked on the door of her house.

"I want to talk to you," she had told me on the phone; it had sounded less like an invitation than a summons. She was talking on the telephone now as she opened the door and stood aside to let me in.

"I don't know, Milton," she said impatiently. "Ought to have worked. You give her two more of the little yellow pills, and one of the capsules. White, speckled, and red."

She waited, while Milton apparently recited back to her the dosages of Agnes Dietrich's medicines. Then she nodded, frowning, spoke a few more words, and hung up.

Except for the phone, walking into Minnie's house was like stepping through a time warp. A cast-iron woodstove hulked in one corner of the parlor, radiating heat in nearly visible waves. In the other corner stood a small spinet; the pages of the music book on it were yellowed and flaking at the edges. Antimacassars lay on the arms and back of the ancient horsehair sofa; across from it, a cricket chair was furnished with a padded footstool, a reading lamp, and a small low table. On the table was an open bag of knitting.

I blinked several times before I realized what was missing: electricity. The lamp was an oil lamp, its glass chimney polished and its wick precisely trimmed. Two more of them were in evidence; one on the spinet, and one on the mantel behind the stove. I glanced sideways through the door that led into the kitchen, and spied the sink.

On it stood a large red hand-pump.

No electricity, and no indoor plumbing, either.

I turned to face Minnie, who evidently read my thoughts.

"I don't need a lot of modern nonsense to be happy," she said. "Only got the telephone when Flanders bullied me. People would be a lot better off if they didn't have to change things every five minutes. Now, sit down."

I perched on the edge of the sofa, whose prickly upholstery made me itch. Minnie's eyes were bright, and as I looked closer, I saw that the brightness came from fury. Pink mottled her cheeks, and her lips were clamped together.

"Minnie, are you all right? Is there something I can do for you?"

"Yes, there is," she said. "I gather you think you're going on with that woman's book."

It took a moment before I realized what she meant. When I did, I tried to explain that it had been my book all along, not Rena's.

"Never mind," she said, gesturing impatiently. Her hand was clean and perfectly manicured, but it looked more like a man's hand than a woman's. Sixty years of farm and garden labor don't discriminate; they put on muscle.

"Heard from that Kilmer woman this morning," she said. "Thought I'd heard the last of her. She said your call put her in mind to talk to me."

Drat the Kilmer woman. She was talkative, all right; a little too talkative for my own good. I opened my mouth to speak, but Minnie got the jump on me.

"All these years," she said angrily, "all these years of peace and quiet." Her gaze darted at me like the sting of a furious wasp.

"I thought," she said, "that it was all over. I thought we put a stop to it, finally, laid all that awful business to rest. But I see I was wrong. You're going to stir it all up again."

"What business? Minnie, that's what I need to know, and if you—"

"Never mind about that. Don't you think I've got enough trouble now? First my dratted nephew, and now this?"

"I was sorry to hear about your nephew—"

She made a noise of disgust. "I should have let him go to an orphanage. I suppose that's all over town by now, too. But at least he's shut away where he belongs. A few other things ought to be shut away, as well." She glared at me.

"Minnie, if you'll just tell me what in the world you're talking about."

She was shaking. A vein pulsed in her throat. All I could think of was what I would do if she had a stroke right here, and me with no car to get her to town. I'd walked here, myself, but I couldn't carry Minnie out.

"I just want you to let well enough alone," she said. "If you must dredge up an old scandal to make a dollar on it, you can at least wait until I'm dead and don't have to know."

"And if I don't wait?" Shockingly, the tone of her voice had implied a threat; I thought I had better find out what the threat was.

"If you don't, whatever you write, I'll simply say you are lying. I'll tell your publisher you've made the whole thing up. I'll fight, I'll sue." She shook a furious finger at me.

"But mainly, girl, I'll ruin you here. I've lived in Pelican Rock all my life, and you're just a youngster, an upstart. How popular do you think you'll be here, after I'm finished with you? Who in town do you think you'll get to give you the time of day, after that?"

"Did you say this to Rena?" I asked.

Her lips tightened. "I would have. I was ready to. But she didn't give me the chance—went and got herself killed before I could talk to her. Not that it would have done any good. She didn't have a lick of sense that I could see. You, though. You're different. Aren't you?"

I glanced away from her angry, demanding gaze. Beyond the window, the ell of the house lengthened into several connected sheds. Through the open shed doors I saw a small tractor, and a potting table with a red gas can and a hose and funnel standing on it. A metal rake leaned against the table, behind which bulked the corner of some larger piece of equipment, neatly covered over with a canvas tarp.

"Minnie, if I promise not to write the book, will you tell me why it's so important that I don't? Not just for me, but for Joey Dolan. He's still missing, and if I understood what's going on, I might be able to find him."

Her face tightened. "That's ridiculous. Your imagination's run away with you. That's the sort of nonsense I want to prevent. You just go along now, and think about what I've said."

I got up and moved toward the door. "If you'd just tell me why."

"Because I'm an old woman," she said as I stepped out onto the porch. "Too old to live down any more talk. All I'm asking is for you to leave an old woman her memories." Then she slammed the door.

I left the porch and went down the front path, leaving behind the brilliant poppies, the picture-book farm so small and neat. The whole place was a living memorial to a way of life that was gone, and she was the curator, defending not just the farm but a whole era.

Looking back, I saw that she had come out again, onto the porch. A chopping block stood there, and as I watched, she picked up a log the size of my arm, hefted an axe, and split the log with a stroke.

She wasn't only strong; she was determined. Whatever Stanley Hardwicke had done or been, I wouldn't find it out from Minnie.

If she had any say in the matter, no one would find it out from me.

And I knew that she'd beaten me with one stroke, too, aiming surely at my most vulnerable spot. Pelican Rock did take care of its own, and Minnie Taylor was more the town's own than I was. When push came to shove, it was Minnie that my neighbors would stick up for, not me.

I walked home, and thought about what life here would be like if I were mistrusted, disliked, grudged against. It wouldn't be pleasant at all. In fact, I probably wouldn't want to live here any more.

Coming down my drive among the fog-slicked bay laurel trees, I looked around at my little cottage, my green dripping yard, and felt things ticking peaceably along. Much of my feeling for the place lay in the neighborly way of life here, the gossip in Arguello's, coffee in the Sea Gull, the small irritations and triumphs of the library and the post office. I liked it. I wanted to keep it, just the way it was.

Which, I realized, was exactly what Minnie Taylor wanted for herself, too.

Right now, however, there was still the small matter of plumbers, and sinks that went whammo.

Or didn't.

When I reached home, I immediately called Harold Flanders again, and this time I got him.

EIGHT

"HAROLD," I SAID. "She'd done the dishes. They were standing on the drainboard. The sponge was damp, there were still a few beads of water in the sink."

"So?" Harold's tone was skeptical.

"So," I said, "I don't think there was anything wrong with it. Or in the bathroom, either—I rinsed my face there."

Yet Dawes had specifically mentioned a leak under a sink. In fact, his whole story that day struck me wrong, now.

I heard the sound of a screen door slamming at Harold's end of the connection. "Just a sec," Harold said to me, and then I heard the voice of Everly Wetmore, one of Harold's ne'er-do-well crew of road workers.

"...goddamn pile of goddamn rocks," he was saying in injured tones, "slidin' back down on the goddamn road ever' time we move the goddamn thang. Can't do 'er with shovels, y'know, we need a goddamn 'dozer, t'do 'er right."

He was, I realized, talking about the slide out on the beach road, near Rena's. About time, I thought. Then another thought twitched at me.

Harold came back on the phone. "I'm sorry, Charlotte. I know you're trying to help. But it doesn't sound to me like...I mean, I can't arrest a guy just for trying to fix something that didn't need to be fixed. Or maybe it did need work, and she used it anyway. But look, I've got my hands full here right now, I've got to go.''

"Okay," I said unhappily. "Sorry I bothered you."

"No bother at all. Don't worry about it. I'll talk to you later." He hung up.

I sat down at the kitchen table, and thought back.

The rain. The silent house. Rena, dead in it. Myself being ill, and phoning Harold, and going outside on the deck to wait for him. Dawes, arriving. His truck, pulling into the sandy drive, coming up beach road, past the sand dunes and the rocks, coming up the road and turning left into Rena's drive.

Turning left. Because he was heading toward town, not away from it. Coming up the road from the highway end, which was closed off.

Coming from the wrong direction. The beach road was closed at the highway end because of the slide that Eberly wanted a bulldozer for. Yet Dawes had come from that end of the road, although he could not have come in from the highway, and although there were no houses with plumbing to fix out beyond Rena's.

Or at Rena's either, I still felt sure.

So what had he been doing?

I grabbed my jacket, stuck a couple of items from the toolbox in my bag, stalked out to the shed, hauled my bicycle from beneath the tarp, wiped the seat with my sleeve, and pedaled off.

If Harold wasn't interested, I was.

Rena's glass doors were impossible, but the front door was equipped with the standard Schlage hardware.

I'd come prepared. It's amazing what you can do with a Case knife and bottle of Elmer's glue. I peeled back the swatch of official yellow paper that sealed the door, popped the lock with a credit card, and went in.

It was quiet inside. The clock had stopped. The curtains were drawn, and the atmosphere was of the tomb, damp and chilly. I padded across the rug to the burnt-wine ceramic tiles of the kitchen ell. It was as I'd told Harold: everything perfect, the counters wiped, the stove-top pristine, dishes still racked in the plastic drainer on the drainboard. There was not a speck of grease or dust to be seen anywhere.

Except under the sink.

Rena was good. She tried hard. To the casual eye, her house was so clean you could use the sink strainer to make your tea. But she was all surface, and so was her place.

The newspapers on the floor of the cabinet under Rena's sink were yellow and crumbling. Clay pots were stacked there, and ancient tin cans, and a Brillo pad so rusty it powdered when I touched it. A box of soap flakes lay on its side, its contents spilled and aged to a lumpy crust. Paintbrushes rotted in jars, the turps long gone, and bristles solidified.

Dust stood so thick on the hump of the curving standpipe that it had collapsed of its own weight into something the color and consistency of old felt.

No one had touched it. Not for years. Maybe not since the house was built.

And there was no puddle, no stain, no smell of dampness. No trace of a leak. I tried the faucets. Water gushed out. I turned them off sharply. The water stopped. No telltale thunking of waterhammers in the pipes. Everything worked fine.

I went up the stairs toward the bathroom, carefully not looking toward the bedroom, then glancing at it in spite of myself.

The door stood ajar. In my mind's eye, beyond it, Rena lay splattered and smashed.

Alive, alive-oh.

"Rena," I said aloud, "leave me alone. I'm doing the best I can, for Christ's sake."

My voice bounced back at me from the silent walls. But the haunted sensation faded. I checked out the bathroom: sink, toilet tank, tub.

Nothing wrong here, either.

Dawes Hobbs, I thought, could gape and play the bumpkin all the livelong day. He could say what he liked about sinks and plumbing that went whammo. He could swear up and down on a stack of Bibles a country mile high that he'd been out here to work on the plumbing for good Ol' Miz Blount, but he was lying through his big yellow teeth.

He'd wanted to get into the house, I thought, but not to work. He'd had some other reason.

I went back downstairs to the kitchen, then, and peered once more beneath the sink. As I crouched there, smelling the smells of age and dirt and neglect but not of leakage, the front door—the door that I had come in—opened quietly behind me.

Then, just as quietly, it closed.

"Hello, Dawes," I said.

"H'lo, Miz Kent." He stood in the entry hall, looking sorrowful. His hands were behind his back. The clover and rabbit's foot dangled together from his belt.

He reached out with one hand, toward my bag which was slung over my shoulder. "Give it here, now. Just . . . give it here."

I blinked. "Huh?"

"The book," he said patiently. "The one you took from her. She was bragging on what she'd wrote in it— I heard her in the Sea Gull. I been lookin' for it. Then I saw you had it. Out to your place, I saw it."

Then I understood. The notebook sticking out of my bag was my own: green cardboard covers, plastic dividers. I'd taken it along with me to Minnie's.

But earlier, I had mistaken Rena's for it. Now, I thought, Dawes had mistaken it for Rena's. And he seemed to want it very badly. In fact, he must have followed me out here to get it.

I stood up slowly. "Dawes. Did you kill her?"

He shook his head. Then he took a step toward me, the kind of slow, careful step you take when you mean to catch an unwilling animal, and you don't want it to know you mean to.

"I didn't know what to do when I saw you had it," he said. "Then this morning I was going to take it when you went out, but you keep bringin' it along with you."

"Dawes, this isn't the book you want."

He didn't seem to hear. "I'm lucky, see?" His voice turned childishly proud. "And curious. I look around, like in that cellar. And . . . finder's keepers."

He took another step, his hands dropping to his sides.

Not the hands of a child. Enormous hands. He flexed them unthinkingly, his eyes holding mine.

"Of course you're lucky," I said, easing sideways a fraction. "You're careful, too. You like to make sure things are done right. I saw that yesterday. Dawes, what cellar?"

He shrugged. "Never mind. It's just a lot of old doctor tools down there. And medicine."

His look became sly. "Lots of medicine. But you don't need to know. I got to make sure nobody knows. Only me. And—" His face closed. "Never mind."

But he'd already said it. Doctor tools, I thought. And lots of medicine.

The only medicine noted in Rena's book had been cocaine hydrochloride, purchasable in vials of 25 and one hundred tablets, sixty years ago.

Purchasable, that is, if you were a doctor, like Stanley Hardwicke, who in his later years had gotten twitchy and suspicious of people. Who wandered the streets, accusing strangers of evil doings that nobody had done. Who finally ran off and vanished, after he had become a raving paranoid maniac.

A thin, suspicious maniac, who'd for years had easy access to cocaine—suddenly I wondered if Stanley Hardwicke had kept a secret stash somewhere.

I held out the notebook. "They'll find me, Dawes, and they'll know I told Harold Flanders, he knows you weren't out here to fix anything—"

It didn't matter; Dawes had been pushed to the breaking point. He didn't believe me, or was past caring.

"It's mine," he said, and his voice was the whine of a frustrated child. *"Mine."* Then he lunged at me.

I was strong the way you are strong when you are in terror of your life, but Dawes Hobbs was stronger. He shoved me against the counter with one arm and took something out of his jacket with the other; suddenly, I realized what that something was, and for the first time I understood that he meant to kill me, here and now.

Outside, a car pulled up. Footsteps mounted the redwood deck, crossed it, and paused.

Dawes glanced uncertainly that way, and in that moment I squirmed away from him; he swung the hand with the gun in it after me, then at the front door.

It opened. Harold Flanders stepped in, saw us, and stopped.

Everything can be fixed, his cautious expression seemed to say, this is bad, it's very bad, but we can talk about it, we can work it out.

"You know, Charlotte," he said. "After I talked to you, I just got an awful feeling. Like maybe I should have listened. I thought you'd most likely just come out here without me. Yes, sir, I thought—"

Then everything happened at once: Dawes fired at Harold, and at me. Diving away too late, Harold grimaced and seemed to lose his footing; I heard the solid *chunk* of his head hitting the corner of the fireplace.

Then a giant slugged me in the chest.

Dawes must have thought he'd killed both of us, or perhaps he was too panicked to make sure, for in a moment I heard the thud of his footsteps pounding across the deck, the roar of the van as he pulled onto the road and sped away.

I lay on the floor, with no particular interest in stopping him. I had, in fact, no particular interest in anything at all. Everything around me was expanding and contracting in a way that I found sickening in the extreme; I thought it very unfair that my dying moments should be so full of nausea. My shirt was warm and wet and sticky, and it smelled like bloody meat.

What they don't tell you about getting shot is the shock it delivers to your nervous system. I imagine it is somewhat like getting smacked broadside with a two-by-four that is swung by a twenty-foot gorilla. The result is stunned paralysis, while a frantic internal inventory is taken. Moreover, the human body when punctured apparently sends blood rushing out to the hands and feet, where it is in less danger of leaking through the new hole.

This, of course, creates temporary scarcity in the brain, which is ordinarily of no account since the brain is processing damage reports and has shut all its other functions down.

I was sure there was something I ought to do. Something important. My brain and body paid no attention. They seemed to feel that I had gotten all of us into this in the first place, and ought to shut up.

I kept trying to focus, to stop the pulsing all around me, but it kept on, fast and red, getting bigger.

Then it slowed. Finally it stopped. Everything, in fact, was slowing down, easing off, mellowing out. It was okay. I took a deep breath. It was wet and bubbly, like breathing underwater.

I considered this with great interest. It was more pleasant than any other topics I could find. Perhaps, I thought, I really was underwater, and this was a dream. Perhaps I was a fish, dreaming a watery dream of being human.

Caught. Gut-hooked.

Rena's telephone was a wall-mounted job above the counter. I reached for it and began to giggle at the ridiculous distance between it and my hand.

I raised my head swimmingly from the floor, and waited. The floor rippled curiously but showed no sign of trying to buck me off. I climbed to my knees and paused again. So far, so good. The red bees swarming behind my eyes kept their humming distance.

I got my elbow onto the counter and grabbed the receiver and sat down hard, and it turned out to be the kind with the push-buttons built right into the trimline handset. Trust Rena to have the latest thing.

It was still connected. There was a sticker pasted to the base; it read: POLICE—FIRE—EMERGENCY. I pushed the first two buttons. I was going to push the next ones, but my fingers did not cooperate. While I tried to remember how to make them work, the damned floor got all twitchy again and began to shake itself up and down.

"Help," I think I managed to say, although no one was listening. Then the floor swung up—aggressive bastard, I remember thinking—and knocked my block off.

I AWOKE IN THE hospital, full of the strong sensation that I had lost something important. Then I remembered, and wished I hadn't.

"Miss Kent, you are an extremely fortunate young woman," said the white-coated young man gazing at me from the foot of the high side-railed bed.

I could have argued with him on that, but decided not to.

"One quarter-inch." He held his fingers apart to demonstrate. "This much to the left, and I'm afraid you wouldn't be looking at me now."

I didn't want to be looking at him now, but I didn't say that either. Instead, afraid of the answer I'd get, I said, "Harold?"

The fellow at the foot of the bed put the tips of his fingertips together.

"Harold Flanders is transporting a man by the name of Dawes Hobbs over to Ukiah. He said to tell you that. He said he thought that it would make you feel better."

I started to cry. It hurt; it hurt a lot. But I didn't care.

"You mean he's not—"

The white-coated young man grinned down at me. "Unh-unh." he said. "Not by a long shot, if you'll forgive the pun."

I did. At that moment, I would have forgiven him absolutely anything.

"Apparently he came to," the doctor—his name tag said he was Dr. Solli—went on, "and found you passed out—he brought you in here. I told him it would make me happy if he came in, too—he has a big wet lump on his head and a nasty bullet hole in his shoulder. But he was stubborn about it, demanded that I just clean him up and let him go."

Suddenly I thought it might be worth living after all.

"So what did you do," I asked Solli, "to put me back together again?"

Dr. Solli grinned, looking extremely pleased with himself. "Oh, not a whole lot. A little cutting, a little sewing. You'd bled some, but nothing major got hit."

"Good," I told him. "I'm going home." I sat up straight and the room took a sudden loop-de-loop.

"Now wait a minute." He frowned in alarm. "This is not just a flesh wound—Harold got off easy, but you didn't. You're barely out of anesthesia. You'll stay here in bed for a couple of days, we'll walk you around some, get you stronger—*then* we'll talk about going home."

"I've got an appointment tomorrow with my publisher," I said. "He's coming from New York, he'll be here one day, and if I don't see him I'm going to be on welfare next week."

"So, he can come here."

"No, he can't. He had an early trauma. Hospitals make him convulse." Lies, all lies. If I died tonight, I would go straight to hell.

"Tomorrow," Solli said, looking exasperated. "Get someone to stay with you, and you can go tomorrow, *if* you promise to take it very easy. I'm lazy, see. I don't like to stitch things I've already stitched before."

Hospitals are like home in only one way: when you want to leave, they have to let you go; that is, if you're actually able to go. Something kept nagging at the back of my mind, but I couldn't catch it. It would come clear, I thought, if I could just get into my own bed, or in fact any bed but this one. Side-rails and bedpans make me irritable.

"By the way," Solli said, eyeing me acutely, "do you have any medical insurance?"

"No." Good going Charlotte, I thought bitterly. "Does that mean you're going to take the stitches back?"

"Very funny. No, it means I'm going to adjust my fee. The hospital's going to charge you for O.R., anesthesia, medication, and the room. X-rays, blood work, too. You're a writer, aren't you?"

I admitted it. Meanwhile, I kept staring at his name tag. Solli; I'd heard that somewhere before, I was sure.

"Wrote all those home repair books?"

I admitted that, too. Then it hit me. Solli. Harold's friend, the one he tried to set me up with.

"You know," I said, "this is one hell of a first date."

Solli laughed. He had a good laugh; just right, in fact.

"We'll try to make up for it later, okay? I liked your books, by the way," he said.

All of a sudden I liked him even more.

"Harold told me about you," he went on, "put me onto the *Home Digest* things. Saved me a lot of money. You know, I've tried my hand at writing. Health advice, things like that. Maybe when you're feeling better you could take a look at what I've done."

I supposed aloud that I probably could.

"Good," he said. "Then maybe we could work on this on the barter system. You give me a little professional advice, and I give you a little professional surgery. And maybe dinner, when you're up to it. Deal?"

Sudden tears came brimming out of my eyes. "That's very kind of you."

Solli grinned again. He was a smily sort of guy.

"You won't think so," he said, "when you see my manuscripts."

"And I can leave tomorrow?"

He looked at me appraisingly. "*If* you're not bleeding, and if you haven't got a fever, and if you're taking good fluids, and if you can walk all the way down the corridor and back without falling down, we'll talk about it," he said.

This last requirement gave me some pause. Just at the moment, a trip to the bathroom seemed like an expedition requiring pack animals and a Sherpa guide.

"I want to get up," I said, and Solli backed away.

"Sorry, not in my job description. I'll get a nurse."

He got two of them, actually, and they bore my wobbly carcass into the small, tiled cubicle and back. My legs felt like plastic sacks filled with half-set jello; my head sat on top of my body with a tentative air, as if it might fall off, or sail away.

But by the next morning I could stagger through Solli's gauntlet; coming back down the corridor, I only clutched the wall once. The sensation of having forgotten something was now almost more painful than my incision.

"Okay," Solli said doubtfully. "But you take it easy, hear? Eat, and sleep, and for God's sake don't tear those stitches. I'm not giving you any more free operations."

I agreed that I would, and would, and wouldn't. I promised to accept a dinner invitation, as soon as I could sit through dinner without wanting to lie down for a nap. Then I called Fort Bragg's only taxi service and paid out fifteen dollars for the ride to Pelican Rock, to Peter's apartment. All romantic questions aside, he was a friend, and more than anything right now I needed my friends. There had been no answer when I phoned, but I was sure he would put me up for a couple of days.

I thanked the driver, and got out. There were thirteen steps in the outside stairway to Peter's apartment. I took them carefully, very slowly, one at a time. I still had a key, and I let myself in with a feeling of intense relief.

Inside, I blinked, looked around, looked again. At first I thought that he had simply rearranged things, perhaps moved the collection of miniature portraits from the kitchen to the hall, where they would show to better advantage.

The wall there, however, was bare too.

Then I thought he'd been robbed. His gold pocket watch was gone from its usual spot on the bedside table; gone, too, were his Indian nickel collection, the tiny Picasso sketch he'd prized, and the silver-and-turquoise cuff links that I had given to him for his birthday.

Nothing like a spot of petty crime, I thought, to improve an already rotten day. I tottered to the wicker chair at the foot of the bed, and let myself down. Maybe Solli was right about staying another day in his hotel; I was already exhausted.

Sitting there, I looked at the hook on Peter's closet door. Something was missing from it, too: Peter's bathrobe. The door looked naked without it.

It wasn't in the bathroom; I had already peered in there, and I doubted very much that Peter had gone out wearing it. So where was it?

Not in the laundry. Peter was a creature of habit. He did his wash, like clockwork, each Friday morning. This wasn't it.

A cold, unpleasant suspicion struck me. I reached out stiffly and opened Peter's bureau drawer, the one where he kept his underwear, socks, and clean handkerchiefs.

Empty. The others, too. The closet held half a dozen wire hangers, all vacant of shirts, and an empty shoebox.

Peter was gone.

I CALLED HAROLD FLANDERS and got his wife, Polly; no, he wasn't home; he'd had to go back over to

Ukiah. No, she didn't know for sure when he would be back; this evening, she thought. Yes, of course she would tell him I'd called, and she knew that he wanted to talk to me. Where was I, and did I need anything?

No, I said, I didn't need anything, but that did not prevent her from sending over a cauliflower-cheese pie, baked in one of her famous potato crusts and accompanied by a bottle of wine and a carton of sour cream.

Word got around awfully fast that I was out of the hospital and holed up at Peter's apartment. Or ex-apartment. Martin McGregor came up with my mail and a chocolate cake, and in return I offered him an exclusive for his column.

"When you feel better," he said gruffly, and I turned away so he wouldn't see me cry. Rose Arguello sent her littlest boy, who presented me with an electric heating pad and inquired in a small voice if getting shot really hurt very much. I said it did, and he should avoid it if he could, and he promised to.

As he was leaving, the phone rang and it was Minnie Taylor. She was sorry about the tone of our discussion the other day, she said; she hoped I understood she had been upset. We could discuss it all again when I had mended. Also, she had been over to my place and fed Ninki; she was in town now, and could she do anything more for me? I asked if she would pick up my prescriptions: codeine, and several antibiotics that Solli insisted I take.

She would, and she did. Twenty minutes later she arrived, wearing a navy wool cape and the navy beret that made her hair look so crisply white. She carried a string net shopping bag and a bundle of her flamboyant yellow-orange poppies, which she arranged in an old mayonnaise jar from under the sink.

Her cheeks were pink, her eyes bright, her hands strong and capable as she set out the little bottles from Swann's Pharmacy. Without much apparent effort at all, she also got the stove in the kitchen going, and stacked an evening's supply of wood on the kitchen table because I could not bend over to get it from the floor.

I tried to thank her and tell her I had given up the Hardwicke book. For I had given it up, I realized now, and I wanted to set her at ease on that score.

"Never mind it," she said. She seemed more subdued than usual, sadly viewing my stiff attempts at movement as if they pained her. "You've been through a good deal on that little boy's account, haven't you? The Dolan boy, I mean."

Surprised, I agreed that one way and another, I had.

"You care about him, I suppose. You must, to do so much."

I nodded. "It probably sounds foolish to you. I mean, the way I've gotten so involved. And I haven't even done him any good."

She gazed at me thoughtfully. "No," she said. "It doesn't sound foolish, and I think you probably have done some good. I think, in fact, that he will be found."

"But how?" I leaned forward, winced, and settled back into my chair. "I don't know anything more now than I did. I just got all caught up in my own theory and never found Joey at all.

"Probably," I concluded miserably, "Dawes killed him. Or maybe he did just run away on his own."

Minnie shook her head. "Dawes Hobbs didn't kill that boy," she said. "I'm certain of it. He'll be found. Mark my words."

I tried to get up, but she gestured me back. "Everything is going to be just fine," she said, sounding so sure of herself that for the moment I believed her, even though I knew she was only trying to make me feel better. It was, I supposed, all those years of nursing that gave her voice such conviction.

But once she had gone, the effect dwindled. Minnie's professional reassurances notwithstanding, I didn't see how things would be all right. I didn't see it at all, and there wasn't a thing I could do but wait, and wonder.

The Sea Gull sent up a bottle of brandy, compliments of the house, and I combined this judiciously with the codeine tablets and several cups of coffee from a thermos also provided by the Sea Gull. The codeine-alcohol combination went directly against Solli's orders but the result was salutory, if not very energizing; wrapped in a blanket, with my feet on a stool, I sat in the rocker by the stove and gazed out the window, watching the evening fog roll up Main Street.

Just as well, I thought, that I was in town where everything was so convenient, with people nearby. Everyone was full of the startling kindness that surfaces in small towns whenever someone has trouble; you may believe yourself a loner, anonymous, solitary, but your neighbors' response to your misfortune will teach you otherwise. It was surprising, and a bit shaming, to discover that although I was a relative newcomer, they did remember me; they did care.

Some of them did, at any rate. Peter had told no one he was leaving and had left no message. To comfort myself, I tried to rock and discovered that the motion pulled nastily at my stitches.

Time for more medicine, I thought, and reached out my hand for the pills on the table.

Then I pulled it back.

Medicine.

That was what I had forgotten: medicine in the cellar. Dawes had said there was medicine; it was his, and he was keeping it for himself.

Harold Flanders must have picked him up before he could get to it.

Considering what had happened the last time I remembered a fact about Dawes Hobbs, I supposed I ought to just stay put and wait for Harold. But suddenly I thought I knew where Joey might be.

Cellars, I thought, make such good hiding places. Cursing myself for stupidity, I left the codeine where it was, and hobbled to the telephone.

"Polly," I said, when she had inquired how I felt now and I said I was fine and she said that she had made chicken soup; if the casserole was too heavy for me I could have broth with escarole, "Polly, did Harold happen to mention *where* he found Dawes Hobbs? Where exactly did he arrest him?"

"Where? Well, my goodness, I think he did, but . . . let me see. Where. On Albion Street, I guess it was."

"Albion Street," I repeated dumbly. Of course.

"Yes, I remember now," Polly went on. "He told me the boy—of course, he's not a boy, is he? Dawes is twenty-five, at least—anyway, he tried to run and Harold had to chase across that muddy lot . . . you know the vacant lot I mean, behind Agnes's house?"

I said I did, and Polly continued.

"He said he thought Dawes had been trying to get into the cellar."

"The cellar," I repeated.

"Yes. Unfortunate creature, I suppose he thought he could hide there. Anyway, it's over now," she said, and I agreed that it was, trying to sound sincere.

"By the way," she said as I was about to hang up, "Harold phoned. The Dodge had a flat, and he won't be back until late. He asked me to tell you not to budge, but I don't suppose you would have, anyway."

I agreed that of course I would not, and we hung up in a glow of mutual good feelings, part of them feigned on my part as I tried not to let her know I was trying hard to get rid of her.

I got out of the rocking chair, wincing and holding onto my side, and put my feet into my shoes, which luckily did not require lacing. It made me feel bad, lying to Polly. It was dark out, damp and getting cold, and I probably did belong in bed with a nice hot cup of chicken broth. But budging—the sooner, the better, I thought—was just exactly what I was going to do. Joey's life might depend on it.

If he still had one.

It did occur to me to call somebody else; one of the men from the fire crew, for instance, would have helped me. I was horribly sure of what I would find in Agnes Dietrich's cellar.

If Joey were down there alive, I was sure, someone would have heard him. No one had.

Which meant he wasn't.

I had just about decided to stagger down into the Sea Gull and ask someone there to help, when the door to the outside stairway opened, and it was Peter.

"What the hell are you doing here?" he said, his voice low and furious.

"Where the hell have you been, is a better question. The apartment's empty..." I waved my hand, and caught hold of a chair.

Then I let go, and he caught me.

Quickly, I told him what had happened and what I'd been thinking, my idea about where Joey was, and what I had to do. I didn't care now if he was angry, or why. I only cared that his arm was around me, supporting me. He gave me an odd look when I'd finished, but he didn't ask any questions, and as we made our way down the stairs, I did my damned best to appear as if I wouldn't fall if he let go.

"So why's your apartment empty?"

"I cleared out this morning," he said. "Then just now I saw the light and came to check it out. It never occurred to me that you'd be here."

He didn't sound as if it were the most welcome discovery he'd ever made in his life. But we were on the sidewalk now and walking in the direction I wanted to go, so I let it pass. After a few more steps and a few deep gulps of foggy air, I seemed to get my second wind.

We turned the corner onto Albion Street.

"My car's up here," he said.

I looked at him in the murky shine of one of Pelican Rock's few streetlights. "Peter, you don't have a car."

"I do now," he said, and his grip on my arm tightened. "I never told you, Charlotte, but you must have known I'd be doing something soon. This is it. I'm going. I'm leaving tonight."

"Without a word to me?"

"I'd have called you."

Somehow I wasn't completely convinced. But I let that pass, too; I'd fight with him, I decided, sometime when I wasn't leaning on him.

Away from the streetlight it was darker. Billows of fog rolled ponderously over the vacant lot behind Agnes Dietrich's house, where a single light glowed in the parlor. Beyond the pickets lay Hillside Cemetery, its markers seeming to stand silent watch in the darkness. The fog prowled among them, thinning to reveal a leaning marble cross as white as bone, then swallowing it again.

On the street beyond Agnes's house stood a small light-blue sedan. "That's my car," Peter said. "Come on, I'll take you home—"

I shook my head no. Rummaging in my bag, I pulled out the bottle of brandy I'd brought along and took a warming swig, standing on the last square of the sidewalk and leaning against the wrought-iron gates that led through the fence into Hillside Cemetery. Then I held out the bottle to Peter; he didn't want it.

"Listen," I told him, "I could be wrong. Maybe Joey's not down there after all, but we've got to look."

Peter said nothing.

The air was crisp, full of the smell and taste of sea salt, and the only sound was the distant pounding of waves and the steady drip, drip, drip of moisture in the leaves of the sodden shrubbery, the pattern of it in the foliage of the overgrown daylily thickets.

I pushed away from the pillar of the cemetery gate. Peter took my arm again, but I was feeling considerably better now, and pulled back.

But the sudden movement sent a wave of wooziness through me. The bottle slipped from my hand and shattered on the sidewalk. In the silent evening, the sound seemed loud as a rifle shot.

And when it died away, I heard weeping, a steady, hopeless sobbing like that of a child who has been shut outside for punishment. It seemed to rise out of the ground just beyond the fence, where flat granite slabs marked the more modern graves.

"Peter, do you hear that?"

"Come on," he said, "it's just some animal. This is a crazy idea, Charlotte—"

"It is not an animal. Do you have a flashlight?"

He looked put-upon, but opened the car and produced one from the glovebox.

The sound faded as I searched the rain-slick greenery with the flash, the polished gravestones gleaming with moisture in the yellowish beam. No one was there. It had been a trick of my mind, perhaps, or wet branches creaking as they moved together in the low wind, or even a distant sound oddly carried in the water-saturated night.

I straightened to move on, and the sound came again, very near: weeping.

"Charlotte, I'm telling you—"

"Shh." Suddenly, I realized whose it was, the larger granite monument whose carved fleur-de-lis pattern was discernible even by flashlight. It was an ornate, expensive stone, dwarfing the others by its size and the complexity of its engraving; it stood almost against the fence, between the white pickets and an enormous thicketlike bed of daylilies.

Beneath that stone lay Elmer Wainwright's mother. *She talks to me,* he'd said. *She tells me stories.* But I didn't believe it. Neither did I believe it was Mrs. Wainwright now, sobbing in her grave, and yet the sound seemed to come up from the earth.

I opened the wrought-iron gate and made my way through the sodden grass. The weeping grew louder, though distant still, as if the child were sobbing from the bottom of a well. Daylilies clustered thick about the Wainwright grave, their saber-shaped leaves drooping heavily over the marker. Water dripped from them and trickled down into the deeply-etched letters that spelled out "Mother."

The sound came from just behind the stone.

Poor Elmer, I thought; he wasn't crazy after all— just sentimental, and not very bright. Dead people didn't tell stories or give advice, and they did not weep aloud. The dead were beyond all these things.

Only the living wept.

I pushed among the daylilies which grew in massed clumps thick enough to hide anything lying on the earth or set into it. Their tuberous roots were a solid mass, woody clusters twisted about each other and in some places pushed halfway up out of the earth by their own growth.

But at the center of the lily bed, no roots pushed up. Dead leaves lay in a flat, rain-soaked mass, but no plants grew in this spot, which was perhaps a foot square. The lilies massed so thick and lush all around that from the edge of the bed one could not see that this small area was vacant.

I pulled at the mat of thin dead foliage. A corner came away, and at once the weeping grew louder. The voice was a child's.

Beneath the mat of leaves I could see a rusted grate. "Joey!"

The weeping stopped.

"Joey, it's me, Charlotte. Are you all right?"

The silence went on so long that I began to be afraid for him; then his voice came again, distantly as if he were at the end of a long tunnel.

"Charlotte. It's dark, I can't get out. The door is locked, I'm locked in—"

"Joey, listen to me. Where are you? What door? How did you get down there?"

He began to sob again. "The cellar," he wept, "I'm in Mrs. Dietrich's cellar, only there's a big door and it's locked and I'm all tied up."

"Okay, okay, just sit tight. I'm coming to get you out."

His cries intensified, as if the possibility of being saved only made him more frightened that he might not be.

"Just stay still! Don't do anything! You're not going to hear me for awhile, Joey, but don't be afraid. I'm on my way, all right? Joey? I'm coming, okay?"

The steady sound of his terrified sobbing was the only reply.

Throughout all of this, Peter watched silently, but I was past worrying about his opinion now. It was not until I reached Agnes's front walk that a thought struck me.

"Peter, why didn't you tell me Rena'd been bragging in the Sea Gull? Dawes said Rena was down there talking about something she'd found out and written in her notebook. Why didn't you tell me?"

I looked back for his reply and saw something interesting.

Rather, what I didn't see was interesting.

I didn't see any windows of Peter's apartment. From where I stood, the corner of Arguello's store hid the whole of the Sea Gull, including the top floor where Peter lived.

Had lived.

Suddenly I felt his eyes on me. I kept walking, looking back toward the Sea Gull every few steps.

I didn't see the light I'd left on in Peter's apartment until I got to Agnes Dietrich's front porch.

Which was where he'd have had to be to see it, too.

"Peter?" I said.

Suddenly he was right behind me, opening the front door, his grip firm on my arm. Very firm.

That was just one more of the wonderful things about Pelican Rock: outside of tourist season, anyway, most people didn't bother locking up.

I wished Agnes had, as before I could even think to scream, Peter pushed me inside.

NINE

"WHAT THE HELL do you think you're doing?"

I tried to pull away, couldn't, and couldn't quite believe how frightened I was of him all at once. Meanwhile, he propelled me wordlessly through the vacant parlor.

The house was cold. Ashes stirred faintly in the draft of the open damper, in the tiled fireplace. The fire in the kitchen stove was dead. A note from Milton, addressed to Minnie was on the table; Peter stopped to read it, still gripping my arm. It said Milton had taken his mother to Willits to see a doctor there, since "the medicines she got hereabouts only made her worse."

Peter frowned.

"Come on," he said, yanking open the cellar door and pushing me down through it. "You know, you've made things a whole lot harder with your damned snooping around."

"What are you talking about? Peter, you're not involved in this, are you? Tell me you're not."

I stumbled on the bottom step and he jerked me to my feet. "Just walk, Charlotte, will you?"

A faint cry came from somewhere beyond the enormous chiffonier that seemed to take up one whole corner of the cellar. The moldy reek of age and decay was thick in the air, the smell of dry-rotted horsehair and old books left to be eaten by worms.

"I'll be damned," Peter said. "He is here. Go on, open it."

Inside the cabinet stood shelf after shelf, row on row of small brown glass vials, each marked with the formula I'd seen before, and the notation "2 grains." Here was Dawes's "medicine," unknown and unremarked-upon for sixty years, a silent testimony to Stanley Hardwicke's fear.

If the stories were true, he had died mad, the victim of a drug-induced psychosis. But like all psychotics, he had real fears, too, and one fear that overpowered them all. He shared it with every addict that has ever lived.

More than anything else, he feared running out of drugs. But unlike most addicts, he could combat that fear. He could simply buy more. Different addresses, assumed names—even then he must have had to take some precautions.

But if each vial contained one hundred pills, I thought the chiffonier must hold perhaps fifty thousand tablets of cocaine hydrochloride, enough to give the most desperate dope fiend at least temporary confidence.

It occurred to me now that this much drug would provide another kind of security, the kind that came from having several hundred thousand dollars' worth of a very popular substance. Of course, that security would vanish if someone—Rena, for example—directed attention toward this cellar before someone else, Dawes Hobbs, for example, could get the goods safely out of the way.

Or Dawes Hobbs and Peter Ross.

They must have been ready to move it when they heard her talking. And they couldn't move it, of course, until they found out if she'd seen it, too.

"Peter?"

He shook his head. "Go on. You wanted the kid—now you've found him."

Joey cried out again. His voice seemed to come from the back of the huge wooden box. I reached deep into it, past the bottles, and found its rear boards firm. Feeling around it, I touched the stones and mortar of the cellar wall; no stones moved. The wall was solid, and yet on the other side of it, Joey wept.

While Peter watched silently, I closed the doors and played the flashlight over the chiffonier again, and this time I found it: the hook, and the hinged place where the mahogany back met iron plates fastened to the stones. The enormous cabinet slid forward easily.

Behind the chiffonier was a door, a simple wooden door that might have led to a closet or a bedroom. A chain fastened to the rear of the chiffonier and leading through the door apparently allowed the heavy chest to be pulled back into position from the other side, when the door was closed.

Hesitantly, I turned the door handle. The door swung open, revealing the passageway beyond.

Three cement steps led up to a tall, wide tunnel, sloping up and away. Somewhere in the darkness, beyond this dank alley, Joey called out again. His voice sounded frantic.

I peered down the passageway, whose gaslight fittings hung useless now. The plank walls had been white-washed long ago, but were flaking hideously; the tunnel looked like the way into a catacomb.

Peter now stood just outside the tunnel, alongside the chiffonier. He'd been carrying a back-pack, and now I noticed that it was more than large enough to hold all the bottles from the chiffonier.

"Peter," I said.

He sighed in answer. "Charlotte, I'm sorry. But I've made promises."

I took a step toward him. The tunnel seemed all at once very narrow, and I did not like to think how dark it would be, without any lights.

There were several things, in fact, that I did not like thinking of. I stepped toward him again, not to be nearer but in a late, vain attempt to get past him and up the stairs.

He put his hand out. I shrank away from it.

The last thing in the world that I wanted, suddenly, was to be any nearer to Peter Ross.

"And," he went on, "the people I've made those promises to, well, they're not going to let me off them. They're just not."

He advanced on me, holding out both hands as if to ask for my understanding. I did understand, though. Too late.

I wanted to shriek. I wanted to sit down and cry myself comatose. I wanted to pound my head against the stone cellar walls: stupid, stupid. Most of all, I wanted to kill him, for betraying me and making me live these moments and know this awful thing about him.

But I wasn't going to kill him. He was going to kill me, instead.

"Peter—"

"If you'd just stayed home, Charlotte. Or stayed anywhere. Away from here. Away."

I didn't want to go away. Especially not where Peter clearly intended to send me. I'd been sleeping with a monster, and I felt as if I'd woken to find a scorpion on my pillow.

"Think," I said. "You don't have to do this."

His eyes had never looked so blue; his smile had never seemed so unprotectedly honest as it did in that moment, because it was honest. I was seeing him clear, for the first time.

No questions, no strings. I'd looked in those eyes a hundred times, never seeing what was there: ice. Easy come, easy go. I'd thought it myself; I'd thought it about him. But I'd never really understood what that meant, until I saw him thinking it about me.

I wasn't a person. He was the person. I was the bit player in his play. No questions, no strings—except the one slowly tightening now around my neck.

"Oh, I'm afraid so," he said. "I do have to do it. You know you could never let me get away with this, if I don't. You do try, Charlotte, I'll give you that much. But in the end, you're such a boring little moralist. I'm sorry, you know. I really am."

"You didn't...kill Rena yourself, did you? Tell me that much."

He relented slightly, looking amused. "Me? Of course not. I didn't even know she was dead until someone told me."

"Dawes killed her, then."

Peter smiled. I'd always liked his smile.

I didn't like it now.

"Had to be. He says no, but who else? Almost blew the whole thing. I told him to go out there and get the notebook. I didn't know he'd take it like a command from God. I figured I'd come on to her a little, myself, too—see if I could find out how much she knew, that way. Only I guess he got too determined about the whole thing, and—''

He shrugged. ''Now, though, it's probably lucky for me he's so stubborn.''

His grin broadened. ''Yeah, I think old Dawes'll keep his mouth shut long enough for me to split. Sometimes it's convenient, him being so dumb. And so bullheaded.''

''He'll tell them sooner or later,'' I said. ''They must be grilling him right this minute.''

''He hasn't talked yet, that's all I care about. Later's fine. By the time anyone finds you here, I'll be long gone.''

So he didn't mean to kill me outright. It was slim comfort; very slim.

''I'll never be an artist,'' he went on. ''I'll just be struggling. Scrambling for time, scrabbling for a buck. Tending bar and sucking up to jerks like Aaron Williams. Unless I take my chance.''

He took a step toward me. ''This is my chance, Charlotte, and I'm taking it.''

Then he did the thing I never could imagine him doing, because I had loved him instead of looking at him, instead of seeing what he was.

He shoved me, hard.

My back slammed the stone wall as I fell. As I struggled up, the door was closing. The chiffonier thudded up against it. The big hook snapped sharply as he pushed it into place.

''Peter!''

No answer. I heard the sound of bottles being swept off shelves, then a distant series of footsteps as he went back across the cellar.

Then the line of light under the door disappeared. But I still held the flashlight. I didn't think Peter would come back for it, if he even remembered I had it. After all, it wouldn't help me get Joey—or myself—out.

Somewhere behind me, Joey whimpered. I felt bad for him, but I wasn't sure anymore that I could help him.

I wasn't sure I could even move.

In the end, though, I did move. There wasn't any choice. Miserable as I was, I could hardly just lie there and die.

I dragged myself backward, wondering how badly I was damaged while realizing that it probably didn't matter. Suddenly it struck me that I had not heard any sound but my own struggling for a while.

"Joey?"

No answer.

I hauled myself up to my feet. Despite ominous sensations from my chest, nothing actually spilled out, so for the time being I counted myself ahead of the game. I went up the steps and into the tunnel. A little way along, the flashlight showed the tunnel opening into a small room whose walls, like those of the passage, were whitewashed planks. Looming eerily in the dim, yellow beam, a glass-fronted cabinet and a rectangular table stood in one corner, flanked by a pair of old soapstone sinks. The floor had settled unevenly, sloping away in two directions: back down the tunnel from which I had come, and into a smaller closetlike chamber at the lowest corner of this room.

From the chamber came a low, drowned burble. I aimed the flash and moved toward the sound. In the floor was a cistern. Something floated awfully in it, something that looked like two pale mittens cast into a patch of dark seaweed.

They were Joey's hand, and Joey's hair.

The cellar was dry, even after weeks of rain. Probably the pipe to the cistern had clogged over the years, permitting only a trickle of water to pass through.

Now, though, something—Joey's renewed struggles, perhaps—had dislodged whatever clogged the pipe. The cistern was full. Joey was drowning.

I bent and grasped the dark floating thatch of Joey's hair and pulled up hard. His face, bloodlessly pale, rose above the water. He was unconscious, his half-open eyes rolled back. Water ran from his nose and mouth.

I slapped him. His eyelids fluttered sluggishly. I slapped him again. He took a halting breath, gagged, and breathed again.

His hands still floated. Raw purple scrapes ringed his wrists where he had worked them against his bonds. A long ragged cut, puckered and water-bleached, ran the length of his skinny forearm; that axe, I thought with a burst of sudden cold fury.

Somehow he had managed to drag his hands free, but the water had risen too fast after that. If I let go of his hair to find where else he had been tied, his face would fall back in the water, and he would drown.

If I didn't try, he would drown anyway.

I slapped him again. His head lolled sideways, but his eyes came open and focused on me for an instant.

"Breathe, dammit, breathe."

Then I let go, and plunged headfirst into the flooded pit. It was like trying to swim in crushed ice. Feeling blindly around, I caught onto the lower rung of the chair he had been tied to, wedged myself under it, and pushed.

It was hard work, very hard. But it wasn't nearly as hard as watching Joey drown would have been. After what seemed like an hour, the chair rose, teetered, and toppled out of the cistern onto the dry floor. I scrambled up after him.

Joey lay motionless, still tied to the chair. The soaked knots resisted my fingers, and I shone the flashlight around searching for something, anything to cut them. The flash beam reflected from the tall glass-fronted cabinet I'd seen earlier.

Dimly, I glimpsed what was inside.

Instruments. Surgical instruments.

It was locked. I punched the flashlight handle through the glass, put my hand through the hole, and grabbed the scalpel lying there with the other instruments, which looked oddly familiar.

Gynecological instruments.

The tunnel, the table, the secret room.

All at once I thought I knew where those missing girls had gone. At the moment, though, I didn't have time to reflect on it.

Clutching the scalpel, I staggered back and sawed at Joey's ropes. Moments later, he was free. I heaved him over and socked him hard in the solar plexus, and flopped him back onto his belly.

He took a bubbly, hitching breath and heaved up an enormous tide of swallowed water.

I lay there and stared at his face, which was yellow in the flashlight's jaundiced glow. There was nothing more I could do. The only way I was going to get up off that floor myself was if somebody mopped me off

it. He would live, or not. It was up to him. I watched
him for what seemed a very long time.

I don't know if it was the nutritive value of Joey's
habitual diet of Twinkies and soda, or the example
provided by his regular intake of Marvel comics, but
something made Joey Dolan take another soggy, tentative breath. He vomited again, and rolled over onto
his back.

"Joey." I shook him, weakly. "Joey. Hey. You
alive?"

I was, meanwhile, asking myself the same question, and getting an answer in the painful affirma-
tive. Jesus, I thought, when do I get to quit? Sooner
or later, I will just lie down and die.

But apparently not yet. My body continued irrita-
bly to function, my heart pumping blood into my head
in great pulsing throbs. My chest felt as if I had been
run over by a bus. It was a classic case of matter over
mind; the spirit was unwilling, but the flesh was damn-
fool stubborn.

Joey moaned, rolled, and threw up again. He must
have swallowed gallons. Then he raised his head,
coughed, and looked blearily at me.

"That fucking Fred," he said.

I FIGURED THE REST out as we dragged ourselves up
the continuation of the tunnel, toward Hillside Cemetery.

Of course there had to be more to the passageway,
because this place, I realized now, had been an abortion clinic. That was what the instruments had been
for.

And in those days, clearly, the patients did not just
stroll in and out the front door. There had to be an-

other way in and out, to preserve the privacy upon which depended the women's reputations as wives and daughters, or possibly maids and serving girls, and thus their very lives.

There must be a route to the outside, divulged perhaps in private consultation, once Doctor Stanley Hardwicke had assured himself of the lady's need, her trustworthiness, and most of all her ability to pay.

The patients had gotten in, and at least in Doctor Hardwicke's prime, they had departed.

Later, when his hands got shaky, they were not so fortunate. Eliza Tate had stayed, I thought, and so had Cordelia Upson and Margaret Walsh.

A brooch was sold, a nest egg plundered, a dear friend implored. Only then would Doctor Hardwicke reveal to his burdened patient that there was, perhaps, an avenue out of her trouble. Once the lady had been relieved of her difficulty, her lips were sealed, unless of course some trusted woman friend should reveal, in strictest confidence, similar grief. Then the clientele enlarged.

The doctor always had the advantage; he might, in the worst case, pull up stakes and move his practice elsewhere. He might be unknown, untried, even disliked. Still he might make his new place, his new living.

To the woman, of course, no such opportunity was available.

But—a way out for her meant a way out for us. A few moments' thought, between jackhammer poundings of the enormous headache I'd developed, and I knew for sure what the way out must be. Exploring the recesses of the chamber by flashlight, I found it.

Getting through it wasn't going to be easy, but somehow I was getting used to that.

"I knew the bastard had something going," Joey said. He meant Fred. I had my arm slung over the kid's shoulder, and he was bearing most of my weight as well as his own, which considering our recent circumstances I thought entirely fair. It was also unavoidable; somewhere in the last few hours I'd lost some of Solli's stitches, along with a good deal of blood.

Joey plodded on gamely. "Guys came to the house a couple of weeks ago," he told me. "It was late at night. In the morning they were gone, but I heard them talking."

We seemed to have been trudging for hours, though I knew we'd come only a hundred feet or so. I hoped intensely that we would reach the exit, with its iron grating cover, very soon.

What we would do then I wasn't sure.

"Fred told this guy all he had to do was put some people in touch," Joey went on, "and it was worth a lot of money. And the guy said, what kind of people? So Fred says to the guy, big people, the kind of people I don't want to know anything about, but this friend of mine does."

The kind of people, I thought, who could take a couple million dollars' worth of drugs off your hands. Fred was right. He didn't want to know them.

"But how the hell did you get in on all this?"

He turned to me, his face eerie in the reflected flash, but I was looking past him, at the cavelike niche in the tunnel wall.

And at the box in it. The box was draped with a heavy black cloth, and scattered over the cloth were several dozen huge orange California poppies, barely wilted.

I pulled the cloth aside. Joey moaned and a shudder went up my own spine as the searching flash beam lit up Stanley Hardwicke's mortal remains. From the portrait upstairs I recognized his signet ring, on the bones that were all that were left of his right hand.

I looked at it, and then back at the poppies, the hugely brilliant multiflora blossoms. And suddenly, with the force of revelation, I knew who had murdered Rena Blount.

"It was Miss Taylor," Joey was saying. "I saw her out on the beach road, and later she came out to your place where I was chopping wood. She had my gun, and she grabbed the axe away from me. It cut me. Later she must have put something in the soda she gave me, because I went to sleep. And when I woke up, I was down here, tied up. She came back and gave me water sometimes, and I think it had sleeping pills in it too, but then after awhile she stopped coming. Listen, can we stop for a while? I don't feel so good."

We had reached the end of the passageway.

"Sure, okay." I didn't feel so good, either, and from the looks of the project still remaining to us, I was going to feel worse.

Short redwood slabs formed a sharply ascending stair at the end of the tunnel. A curtain of mossy vegetable matter hung down from what I hoped intensely was the grating covering the exit. I remembered the lilies; seen from below, their tuberous roots were like knotty thumbs, bulging through the cobwebby gaps in the old planks bracing the walls.

In the dirt and rotted leaves lying inches deep on the floor all around us, beetles scrabbled, their peaceful digestive processes disturbed by our movements. The flashlight was dying now, and in the fading beam their shiny bodies reflected faintly.

"Yuck," Joey said. I couldn't have agreed with him more. I didn't like thinking about what the beetles were digesting; we were, after all, underground in a graveyard, the earth around us studded with coffins like raisins in a cake.

"Look," I said, "we're going to have to get through that. It's the way out."

Joey shivered.

"Joey, come on. Nothing's as bad as staying here." As I tried to persuade him, I argued also with myself, trying not to imagine the touch of the mossy stuff on my face, the feeling of beetles running on my arms and legs, in the dark.

Joey's look was unconvinced.

"Joey," I said, "we've got to do it. Do it, or die."

And then I wished intently that I had kept my mouth shut. A look of determination came over his sallow face as he straightened his shoulders, stepped over my legs, and grabbed the end of one of the old boards bracing the wall. Before I could stop him, he pulled it away from the crumbling earth, dragged it around, and swung it hard at the grayish canopy hanging above us. It fell in a choking cloud of insects, leaf mold, and dirt.

Suddenly the tunnel was alive with small moving creatures that burrowed against me, in my ears and against my eyelids, across my lips which I bit hard so as not to scream and let them in. The beetle nest had lain here, undisturbed, for years; stirred, its huge, horrid population swarmed over me in scrabbling insectile panic. Through the dust I saw Joey hopping and slapping at himself.

Abruptly he stopped. A puzzled expression replaced the revulsion on his face. He seemed to be listening. Then he leaned forward, grabbed my arm, and pulled hard, while batting with his other hand at a large beetle crawling down his forehead.

"Hey," I said. Then I heard it too: a heavy creaking, splintering sound, the patter of trickling earth and the sharp dry crack of old wood giving way.

Joey had pulled the wrong board, or perhaps any board would have been the wrong one. Fifty years of dry rot, the weight of the earth, and periodic tremblers shuddering up the San Andreas fault hadn't done the tunnel any good.

Now it was caving in.

Joey pushed me up the redwood-slab steps toward the top of the shaft. We reached the top one and huddled on it, while below the rending, rumbling sounds of destruction went on.

The earth at the top of the steps quivered, but held for the moment. Anything, I thought, could bring it down around us. Anything.

Gingerly, I felt above me and found the bars of the grating over the hole.

"Give me the board," I said to Joey. His eyes were hugely dark and frightened in the dying flashlight's glow. Wordlessly, he handed me the stick of wood. I pushed it through the bars, lifting the mat of dry leaves overhead. Fresh air flowed in, smelling of fog and sea salt.

"Okay, this isn't so bad," I said, as much to myself as to Joey. I was bleeding again, warm wetness trickling down my stiff shirtfront, and despite the fresh air

I could not get quite as deep a breath as I seemed to need. Each attempt brought a faint wet ratchety noise from somewhere in my chest.

"See, we'll just push on the grate with the board, and lift it up."

"Uh-oh," Joey said. He had taken the flashlight, and aimed it upward. The beam flickered dimly but I could still make out the frame into which the grating had been laid. Like the steps, it was made of rough-hewn redwood. Heavy iron boltloops protruded from it at all four corners. They had been obscured by the mat of dead leaves, but from this angle I saw them clearly.

Thick chains fastened the grating firmly to them. The chains looked ancient, thickly rusted, but still unbreakable. The board was useless, and so was my escape plan. Nothing short of bolt-cutters would get us out this.

Joey began to cry quietly.

I thought I might, too. Clods of dirt pattered below as the earth settled and made ready to give way again. The earth pressed threateningly around us; one little hiccup of shifting soil and we would be dead.

Then I heard it.

"Shut up," I told Joey.

He looked at me with miserable resentment, sniffled hugely, and was silent. His breath came in little hitching sobs as he struggled for control.

"Why?" he said. "We're trapped here, we're going to die any minute, what's the—"

"Shut *up*. Listen."

He frowned, and did as he was told. At first there was nothing, only the distant sound of waves on the rocks far away, below the bluffs. Then he heard it, too.

"Hey," he said. "Hey, there's somebody out there." Before I could stop him, he pushed his face up to the grate.

"Hey! Hey! Somebody, over here, hey!"

It could have been anyone out there. But it was too late to tell him that. Footsteps approached the grate, accompanied by a steady long-suffering mutter of irritation.

"Now, listen," said a familiar voice. "I hate to say it, but this is getting to be too much. It's just not fair."

The voice came nearer. "I've tried, Lord knows that I have tried. I know you're lonely, and I have done my level best to keep you company. But now I'm going to have to get on with my life. I have things to do too, you know, and I want—"

Beyond the grate, Elmer Wainwright's moonish face appeared, looming above the daylily fronds. He frowned at the earth, seeming to speak directly to it.

"Elmer," Joey yelled. "Elmer, down here!"

A look of absolute confoundment spread across Elmer's features. Crouching, he pushed through the daylily patch and knelt among the fronds, peering down at us, seeming oblivious to the fact of our predicament as his lower lip pushed into a pout of cheated resentment.

"Watch it," I called up to him, "this hole's ready to collapse."

Elmer ignored me, frowning for a long moment as he tried to make sense of what he saw. He looked at us, then at the grating, then again at Joey and me.

"Hey," he said at last. As comprehension dawned, a hint of relief crept into his face. I saw him struggle guiltily with it.

Then he grinned.

"Hey," he said again. "Hey, you're not my mother."

TEN

"OF COURSE," I SAID to Harold. "I ought to have figured it out sooner. Snatching Joey was one thing; that made sense, whoever the killer was. But trying to make it look like Joey murdered Rena was something else. The Deadly Drifter would have made a much better suspect—only he was in jail. And just one person knew that soon enough to make use of the information—Minnie Taylor."

Harold had called Polly and sent Joey home with her; now we were driving very fast up Highway One in the Dodge. One look at me, and Harold had put on the flashing red light on his dashboard and turned the car toward Coast General Hospital.

"How did she know, though?" he said now. "They kept his arrest quiet for over twelve hours, while they questioned him."

I turned to him. "He's her nephew."

Harold nodded. "Yeah. Too bad for her. So what?"

"So," I told him, "they might have kept his arrest quiet, but somebody didn't keep him quiet. Or maybe he telephoned just before they picked him up, I don't know. But I have it on good authority that he always calls his good old auntie when he's in trouble. And this time I'll bet the news was even less welcome than usual to Minnie."

He nodded. "The one I feel sorry for, after Rena, of course, is poor Dawes—except that he shot us, the damn fool. But I'll bet Peter never intended to cut him in on the cocaine deal at all. Right from the beginning, Peter would have been looking for a way to get rid of him. When he heard Dawes had been picked up, he took his chance, left his partner holding the empty bag."

"Dawes wouldn't have had a clue what to do with that much cocaine when he found it," I said. "He must have taken Peter in as a partner. And Peter had heard Fred Dolan talk about the heavy people he knows, and Fred introduced him to someone."

Harold nodded, eyes on the road.

"Then," he said, "it turned out Rena Blount might be a problem. Peter and Dawes had to know if she'd seen the stash before they moved it, because if she had, she'd certainly raise a stink when it disappeared. Then people might start to think about who liked to poke around in cellars."

"And when she turned up dead, Peter thought Dawes killed her."

"Right. So there Peter was," I mused, "with murder on one side and a lot of anxious underworld guys on the other."

It all must have made him very nervous, indeed.

I almost felt sorry for him.

"But why didn't they take the cocaine out of the cellar when Dawes first found it?" I wondered aloud.

"Safest place for it, I'd say, probably," Harold said. "After all, it'd been there sixty years. They didn't want to risk moving it twice. Hell, I sure wouldn't— that's a lot of dope, you'd get a lot of time if you got caught with it. Way he figures it now, though, Peter probably thinks he's got away clean."

"What do you mean, the way he figures it?"

Harold shrugged. "Lot of money involved, for one thing. Who knows how good that stuff really is after sixty years, for another. Probably they tried some, but that doesn't mean all of it's still okay. And even if it is good, Peter Ross is purely a beginner. An amateur. I'm just a country cop, Charlotte, but I know that when amateurs deal with professionals, there's a pattern to the way the deals usually turn out."

"What do you mean?" I gripped the dashboard as the Dodge negotiated a sharp left-hand curve.

Harold glanced sadly at me. "I mean one less amateur," he said.

Just for an instant there, I didn't care how fast we were going. The lights of oncoming cars zoomed up and past, blurred in my tears.

I nodded. Then another thought hit me hard.

"Harold," I said. "Slow down. Turn the car around."

He waved this suggestion away with one hand, then clamped it hastily back onto the steering wheel. It struck me that I'd never known Harold to drive this fast before.

Probably, I realized, he never had. The thought made me even more anxious to get the Dodge's accelerator up off the floorboard. More people die in car crashes than get murdered, I knew, and I was not anxious to validate this statistic.

"Once we tell poor Dawes his partner has split with his treasure, we'll get him talking soon enough," Harold said.

"Harold—" I bit my lip as truck headlights roared up into our windshield and hurtled by.

"Harold, slow down. Find a place to pull in, and turn around. Do it."

"Why?"

"Because I talked to Minnie just before I found Joey, and now I think I know what she meant by what she said."

"I don't care what Minnie meant," Harold said gruffly. "I doubt she's going to go on the run, that's all I care about. I'll deal with her shortly. Right now you're bleeding and I want you in the hospital."

"The way you're driving, I'm more apt to die of a heart attack than anything else. But Harold, I think she's going to kill herself, if she hasn't already. We've got to get out to her place."

The boy will be found, she'd said. Not just to make me feel better, but because she'd already decided to tell where she'd put him.

And knowing what I now knew, I doubted she meant to survive the revelation. Otherwise, she'd have simply told me at once.

She was brave in her way, but I couldn't see her facing the arrest, the publicity, the trial, maybe even jail. I was willing to bet she couldn't see it, either.

And wasn't planning to.

I told Harold all this.

He considered for about sixty seconds, while a mile and a quarter whizzed by. Then he slowed the car.

"Charlotte," he said as he pulled over to the shoulder; gravel sprayed behind us as we swung out again, going the other way. "Charlotte, you know I like you and I think you're pretty smart. I admire that, I really do. You've been a big help to me, and I'm grateful. But I must say, Charlotte—"

He swerved around a slow-moving station wagon and accelerated past it; I caught my breath, which was quite a trick, considering how elusive it was getting.

But I didn't want to tell Harold that.

"I must say," he went on as we careened, siren blaring and red light flashing, back down the highway toward Pelican Rock, "I'm getting awfully tired of you being so blasted right all the gosh-darned time."

"Not as tired as I am, Harold," I said, stomping hard and ineffectually on an imaginary brake pedal. "Not near as tired as I am, believe me."

I LET OUT A PAINFUL sigh of relief as I caught sight of her, and realized we'd gotten to her in time.

We found her in her garden, sitting on the cold, damp ground. The whole place was dark. Wraiths of mist floated in the pasture, where the goats stood neglected and bleating forlornly. In the distance, a foghorn let out its regretful moan.

"Yes, I killed Rena," Minnie said. "You see, I killed Stanley Hardwicke, too, all those years ago. And she would have told."

"If I had known...no," she went on. "I did know. I let it go on. Stanley Hardwicke had always been a good, kind man. But he changed—the drugs changed him. When I found out, found out for sure...and then, they were going to kill him anyway. The fathers of those girls, and the others in town. They wanted to tar him and ride him out on a rail."

Harold half walked, half carried her into the house, lit the lamps, got the fire stoked and the kettle going, all in silence.

"Here," he said at last, handing us both cups of tea.

It was an odd gesture, from a sheriff to a murderess. I supposed he felt as I did. Whatever we now knew, it was hard to think of her that way.

"Not his wives," I said. "That's what Agnes tried to tell me—no one really thought he'd killed his wives, and he didn't. It was the other girls people found out about, later—the ones who died of his botched abortions."

"Exactly," she replied. "Oh, he put one over on all of us. Such a tragic figure, such a hero! And all the while, at night, in the dark..."

She sipped her tea, and looked straight at me. "Of course, everything is different now. Now the girls go into the hospital, and insurance pays for everything. But in those days, when a girl was in trouble..."

"Stanley Hardwicke got them out of it."

She nodded grimly. "Indeed he would. Got them out of all the trouble they might ever see again. I suppose he did some of them all right... otherwise, how could he keep on? But when his hands began shaking, and he couldn't practice upstairs anymore, he kept right at it."

"But how did anyone find out?"

She shook her head. "That I don't know. When the last of the girls disappeared—Margaret Walsh, that was—one of her friends, I suppose, must have been in on the secret. And she told someone, and someone told somebody else. And in a few days, this town was a mob. What they wanted to do...we couldn't let that happen."

She looked at her hands. They weren't shaking anymore, and her voice was calmer. "I couldn't let it happen," she said. "I loved him, you see. It was against my better judgment, but I always, always loved him."

"Who else knew?" I asked.

"Just the Jackson girls, Agnes, and myself. We hid him. Tied him, and hid him. And it worked, too. For a while."

"And then?" Harold put in.

She stopped, her eyes focused on nothing. She seemed to be looking backward in time.

"Then I put an end to it. He was mad. I went down one day, and found him lying there in filth. And I just couldn't stand to see him that way any more. My brother had been killed in an accident on a ship, and I got a settlement. I had a chance to close that madhouse, and I did. I killed Stanley Hardwicke. I overdosed him with those drugs of his and told the others that he'd wandered away. That was the story we'd put out in the first place. And after a while, he was declared dead."

"And Agnes and the Jackson twins inherited everything?"

Minnie nodded, a half-smile on her face. "After all that, he didn't leave me a pin. They knew, of course. They knew what I'd done. I never told them, and they never asked me, but they knew. And they were glad— at least, Beatrice and Rose were."

"And Agnes?"

"Agnes," she said bitterly. "I think she knew, too, but she never said so. She'd never set foot in that cellar—never would. He was a hero to her, she never believed a word against him. Then all these years later the Blount woman had to come around, and Agnes decided to tell her tale."

She paused, sipped at the tea, and put the cup down. "I heard Rena boasting in your workshop," she said to me, "and I went to Agnes at once. But it was too late—she'd already told Rena enough to get it all going. Once she found Rena, you see, she didn't care about you. She knew you'd think of what damage might be caused. But Rena—well, in her Agnes found the perfect vehicle for the revenge she'd wanted so long.

"But I put a stop to that," she went on. "It was too late, of course, but I could keep her from telling it again, at least. If *you* ever want to get in charge of anybody, get in charge of their medicines."

Of course, I thought. Nothing like a triple dose of tranquilizer to make an old woman act senile. Agnes had been fading a bit, but the pills were what made her so much worse, so quickly.

"And Rena?" I prodded. "What about her?"

"Stubborn," Minnie said. "Not like you. I knew you saw reason. But when I told her I wanted those diaries, she just laughed."

"Diaries?" I said. "What diaries? You said there were none. I thought it was her notebook—" I stopped. She hadn't taken the notebook, although she'd had the chance.

"Oh, I didn't care what she wrote," Minnie said. "I could deny that."

She looked down at her hands. "The diaries were different. Agnes told me she'd given them to Rena, so I went out there to get them back."

She made a disgusted face. "And Rena played so polite, at first. Humoring the senior citizen. Made tea, even. I hadn't gone there intending to kill her, but I did have a new prescription for Agnes with me. I'd just picked it up at Swann's. And once I'd decided what to do, I asked to use the bathroom. While I was there, I emptied a lot of the capsules into a tissue."

Eyebrows raised, I looked at Harold. "Toxicology screen on her body's due back today," he said quietly.

Minnie went on as if he hadn't spoken. "When I came back, she was in the kitchen, talking on the telephone. I put the granules into her cup—even then I wasn't sure she'd drink it. Or she might notice—

"But she did drink it, and she didn't notice. Once she was asleep, I strangled her. I had to—the capsule contents might not do it alone, you see. And then, too, I'd read about the Drifter. That was how he did it. But on the way home I was listening for cars, not boys walking. Joey Dolan saw me, and when I did get home, the telephone rang and it was my nephew."

She chuckled brokenly. "It was very odd, I can tell you, first pretending to be the Drifter, then getting a phone call from him. Almost as if . . ."

She stopped, looking down at her hands. Even by lamplight, they were strong hands. Strong as a man's.

I had looked at them before. But I hadn't seen them. The way I hadn't seen Peter: in him, too, I'd seen what I wanted to see, until he nearly killed me.

"So," she finished, "of course I had to fix things. But it turned out I only made them worse. Once the autopsy showed she'd been strangled—well, I'd tried to fix that, too. The shotgun should have done it. But," she ended, "it didn't. My hands were shaking so . . ."

"Minnie," I said, "I still don't understand how Stanley Hardwicke's old diaries could hurt you."

She looked surprised. "But they weren't. They weren't his at all, I told you he never kept one. They were mine, and I'd written how I killed him. Later I threw them in the stove, but Agnes must have been

spying and rescued them somehow, saved them all
these years. Saved them for when they would hurt
worst.''

She shook her head. ''For the rest of my life I'd be
a murderess, and a picturesque one, at that. A curiosity. The gawkers and the tourists—they'd be here,
gawking at me. And I'm too old to live it down, now.''
Her lips twisted on the words; she was silent a moment.

''What changed your mind?'' I asked her quietly.

''It all fell apart. Milton took Agnes away, and once
the tranquilizers wear off, she'll be talking. And then
there's that Dolan boy—what was I to do with him? I
meant to kill him too, you see, I thought I'd have to,
but then—'' She put her hands out in a gesture of
helplessness.

''—Then I talked to you, Charlotte.''

At my puzzled look, she nodded firmly.

''This afternoon, I saw the way *you* were.'' She
looked intently at me. ''What *you'd* gone through,
over that boy—what you'd given up, how hurt you
were. The child couldn't be as worthless as he seemed,
I thought, even with those awful parents of his, if you
cared that much about him. And then, all of a sudden, I was just too tired. Time to stop trying to keep
it all a secret, I thought. Time to let the young ones go
on. So I came home. Home, to rest.''

She frowned suddenly. ''I'm ready to go now,'' she
said, then cocked her head as if listening. A look of
surprised pain came onto her face.

''The diaries, by the way,'' she managed to say. ''I
took them, and I burned them for sure this time.''
Then she collapsed. The note she'd been hiding in one

hand fluttered onto the carpet, along with a small red plastic pill bottle.

The note told where Joey was, or rather, where he had been when she wrote it. The label on the pill bottle read "digitalis."

The bottle itself was empty.

Cursing, Harold snatched both of them up. "Come on, let's get her out to the car." He lifted Minnie easily.

I followed, full of the sudden, bitter realization that once again I'd seen only what I wanted to see. We hadn't been in time, after all.

Or, I thought, maybe we had. Ahead of me, Harold slowed suddenly as he too seemed to realize what we were doing. We hadn't been in time to keep her from trying to kill herself, but what, after all, would we be saving her for? The rest of her life would be a misery, and even after all she'd done, I didn't wish her that.

Harold must have thought the same, for in the end he didn't bother with siren or flasher, and he drove sedately toward Fort Bragg and the hospital.

Very sedately. He had, I realized, known Minnie all his life; she'd been a friend. And Harold wasn't one to go and mess up a friend's decision.

Especially when, in his heart, he agreed with it.

"BUT," SOLLI SAID, as he examined my chest with crushingly impersonal surgeon's interest, "how did Elmer know? You can't tell me his mother whispered it to him from the grave, so how did he find out Rena was strangled?"

"From Minnie herself," I said, suppressing a squeal as Solli's gentle probing hit paydirt. "Joey said she carried on conversations with Hardwicke, as if he were alive. She was down there, haranguing him about what she'd done for him and her voice carried in the tunnel, just like Joey's did when I heard him crying. Ouch."

"Sorry," he said abstractedly.

"As for Dawes, he didn't even know she was dead, at first. When she didn't answer her phone, he thought she was out, so he probably went to look for the notebook. Driving by, he saw her car there, so he went on up the road to turn around. Probably he sat there a few minutes, wondering what to do next. But when he came back, he saw me, and when he saw what he thought was her notebook at my place, he put two and two together."

"And got five," Solli said.

"Right. And came after me. By then he was pushed past all reasoning—what little he had in the first place. He probably thought I killed her, and so I must know enough to screw up his plans, too. Finally Harold showed up, and that freaked him out completely." I winced again.

"Oops," Solli said. "Just a couple more of these little skin sutures to take out."

"You're not under any circumstances supposed to say 'oops' to a patient," I told him.

Solli grinned, keeping his eyes on his work.

"You," he pointed out, "were under no circumstances supposed to rip out these stitches. There's a little tear in your lung which I was hoping would close and reinflate by itself, but now you've rattled it around. It shows on your x-ray, and it's why you're so short on air."

I glanced down, then turned my attention firmly away from what he was doing with a scissors and a curved suture needle. My attention, however, kept getting drawn back.

"Speaking of drugs," I said, "couldn't you give me something to take the edge off what you're doing?"

"You don't need it," Solli said. A lot he knew. "Turn sideways a little."

"Okay. Ouch. Yeah. Criminy, you putting in a hem, or what?"

Solli laughed. "Two more minutes."

He turned away to fuss with something on the gleaming counter of the surgery clinic's examining room.

I took an experimental breath. The stitches pulled, but the unpleasant ragged sensation had disappeared, now that all my parts were reattached to all my other parts. I took in more air, what I could get of it.

It was almost okay. Almost.

"You know, I still can't quite take a deep breath."

"Mmm," Solli said, still turned away. I couldn't see what he was doing. I did notice suddenly, however that there was a good deal more apparatus in this room than I thought Solli had any use for, assuming he was only stitching me together.

"What's that?" I said.

Solli turned. In one gloved hand, he held a small glass hypodermic whose tiny needle resembled a stinger. In the other, he held a large unpleasant-looking instrument which also resembled a stinger, only this stinger came from a mosquito the size of an ox.

"That?" he said, following my gaze to a plastic receptacle hanging by two wire hooks from the side of the stretcher where I lay. Its dual chambers, half full of water, bubbled merrily. A hose led from the chamber to an outlet in the wall. The label on the outlet read "suction."

Solli gave me a smile which I thought was meant to be reassuring, but which failed miserably.

"That's going to help reinflate your lung. Just lie back again, we'll zip this chest tube in and hook it to the suction and you'll be all set."

I looked at the larger of the two skewers he was holding.

"Solli," I said, "tell me the truth. You're not going to poke a hole in my chest with that thing, are you?"

In spite of myself, I was already lying down. I guess they learn that in medical school.

Solli stood by the stretcher and looked down into my eyes.

"Charlotte," he said, "I will tell you the truth. In fact, I am going to poke a hole in your chest with this thing. But believe me, it won't hurt a bit. You'll feel some pressure, and that's all."

Sure, I thought. That's what they all say. I was, however, in no position to argue with him. I was getting shorter of temper, but also shorter and shorter of breath.

"Oh, hell, you're the doctor." I felt the tiny zing of the xylocaine from the hypodermic, then spreading numbness.

"Mmm," Solli said, his eyes intent on my rib cage. "You're right, I am. Try to remember that next time I ask you not to spoil my needlework."

Then he did it. He was quick and deft, and he was right; it didn't hurt. I only felt pressure.

About as much pressure as you would feel from a mosquito the size of an ox.

"I STILL DON'T GET it," Joey complained.

It was two weeks later; I was out of the hospital, on strict orders not to exert myself. Joey was splitting chunks of redwood into stove-sized sticks. I sat in a canvas chair, watching him and enjoying the freakishly early spring sunshine that streamed in pale shafts between the dark-green redwood boughs.

"Don't get what?" I asked. By the time Harold Flanders had gotten the whole story, Fred and Phyliss had departed for places unknown. Liane now lived at the commune where I'd taken her the day we met Kenny Biewald. Joey lived at my place, and when he wasn't in school he spent most of his time here. Sometimes Harold Flanders came out, too, and taught him about gun safety, or took him for rides.

Sooner or later, I supposed, I was probably going to have to adopt him. I could, if I had to, although so far we were doing okay without any official permissions. Harold had told the family court that Joey was all right in my care, and since they really didn't have anything better to do with him, they accepted it.

One way or another, I knew, I wasn't going to let him get into any more hard places. But it seemed we had time to figure out how we were going to arrange that.

I didn't know what had happened to Peter. No one had seen or heard a thing of him. The police theory was that he'd met up with whoever was supposed to buy the cocaine from him.

The theory was that he hadn't survived the encounter.

In my lap lay Kieran Gray's new story, submitted for the workshop, whose next meeting was tonight. Entitled, "Homecoming," it was neatly typed, double-spaced, on good white bond with wide margins and only a very few minor misspellings. Kieran had brought it out himself, muttering shy thanks and departing immediately. It represented a quantum leap for Kieran, and I thought it as good a proof as any that things could change, things could improve.

I hoped it was true.

Joey raised the sledgehammer and brought it down on the wedge with a satisfying thwack. The two halves of the chunk he was splitting flew in opposite directions and he retrieved them.

"I don't get," he said, "why Minnie got so nuts. I mean, you should've heard her, wandering around in that cellar, talking to dead people. Sometimes she'd think I was that old dead guy and start cursing at me. Then other times, she'd bring me water and call me darling."

He pronounced this last word with some difficulty, and made a face. "It was really weird, you know?"

I considered what to say. He'd only recently begun discussing the time he'd spent imprisoned. Clearly, the memories bothered him.

"Well, if you know she was disturbed, what don't you understand? What is it that you really want to know?"

I asked this with some nervousness. There were things I didn't want to try to explain, and Minnie's history was one of them.

Minnie, who loved Stanley Hardwicke with an obsessiveness possible, perhaps, only to a lonely, repressed Victorian girl.

And who hated him, just as obsessively, for disappointing her. I thought of her watching in disgust as he sank into his private hell, and loving him all the more desperately to make up for the secret hate.

I thought of her killing him and taking all the guilt on herself. There was more, I thought, than she had told us. Someone had nursed those wretched women while they died slowly of Hardwicke's botching. Someone had hidden them and kept silent. The Jackson girls, I thought, bore their share of the guilt.

"What do you want to know?" I asked Joey again.

He put down the hammer, and came over to the porch. He'd put on some weight, I thought, and the beaten look was fading from his expression. Still his dark eyes were full of worry.

"Well, Mister Flanders said maybe she had weird experiences when she was a little kid."

I said I thought she very probably had. It was as good a theory as any to explain why she'd been so vulnerable to Hardwicke in the first place.

"And they made her nuts. Is that basically it?"

I temporized here, allowing that they had certainly helped things along.

"But," I added, seeing now where this might be leading, "an unfortunate childhood isn't enough to cause that sort of behavior. At least, I don't think it is. A person would have to be susceptible to start with, I believe."

Really, I thought, I'm not the one to explain this. If I understood, I could win the Nobel prize, instead of trying to make my living writing guides to home repair.

Which it looked as if I was going to be doing. I'd called Bernie. My next opus was entitled *Fun With Formica!*

Joey pressed on, looking troubled.

"*I've* had a weird childhood. You know, my dad taking off, and Fred being the way he is. There's a lot of stuff you don't know about, too."

I'll bet, I thought, with a surge of anger for the absent Fred.

"And—"

Joey lowered his gaze, summoning his courage for the next thing with an effort.

"I think I'm susceptible," he confessed.

He forced his eyes up to meet mine. "I mean, I cry a lot. When I think about things. Like things in the cellar, and—" He stopped and swallowed hard, the newly developed adam's apple bobbing in his gawky neck. "And other things. You know?"

I did know. I thought I might be about to cry any minute, in fact. It hadn't taken much to bring on the floods in the past two weeks, especially.

"I'm afraid maybe I'm going to get nuts, too," Joey said. "Maybe now, or maybe someday. Sometimes I think, when I get crying, that I won't be able to stop. Is there any medicine or anything they can give you, if you can't stop?"

I cleared my throat.

"Yeah," I said. "Yeah, I guess there's medicine. But I don't think you're going to need it."

"You don't?" He wasn't sure whether to believe me.

"Nope. I don't. Remember when we were in that hole?"

"Boy, I sure do." He shivered expressively.

"And I said we had to get out of there? Remember what you did?"

"Yeah." His voice was disgusted. "I nearly killed us both."

"But you didn't know that was going to happen. What you did, Joey, was you tried. You grabbed that board, you didn't care about beetles or anything. It was you who finally got us out of there."

This was not completely true, but the lie was worth it.

Joey looked doubtful.

"But what's that got to do with now? With me crying so much?"

"Um," I said. "Well. When they hauled us out of the hole, you stopped trying, didn't you?"

"Sure I did. I didn't need to try anymore."

"Right. Well, that's it, see. When you didn't need to, you could stop. It's the same with crying."

I hope, I added silently.

He frowned. "Maybe I get it. You mean, I'm not nuts, but I'm just gonna cry until I don't need to cry, too? And then I'll just stop? Like when I'm done?"

I nodded. The morning's mist was steadily burning away, the sunshine pouring down through the branches, smelling of evergreen and salt. Fist-sized buds of rhododendron pushed out between the dark shiny leaves, ready to burst at the slightest excuse.

"Something like that," I said. Beads of dew glittered like diamonds in the cupped blossoms of the primroses. Waves boomed distantly, their heavy sound moving away on an offshore breeze. Foghorns tootled, miles away.

Joey looked relieved. He strode back to the wood-pile and hefted the sledge, wearing a smile that looked new but still had something of cockiness in it.

He positioned a new slab of redwood.

"You mean," he said, "when you gotta try, you gotta try? And when you gotta cry, you gotta cry?"

He swung the sledge. It struck the wedge ringingly, in the new sweet-smelling sunlight. The halves of wood flew brightly away into the grass.

"Right," I said. "Right, that's exactly it."

Joey lifted the hammer again, repeating his phrase to himself. Then he looked at me.

"Hey," he said in a wondering voice. His smile was less tentative now. With practice, I thought, he might get good at it.

"Hey," he said again. "Guess what? I'm a poet!"

A JOANNA STARK MYSTERY

DARK STAR

MARCIA MULLER

A splash of red. From her peaceful Sonoma Valley home, art-security expert Joanna Stark can't escape the crippling fear that Antony Parducci—thief, art dealer, dreaded enemy and onetime lover—is nearby, hot on the trail of a newly discovered Van Gogh. Then a worthless but significant painting suddenly disappears from Joanna's own collection and she knows Parducci has left his calling card...challenging her to a deadly game of cat and mouse.

But when Parducci's dead body is found splayed in her living room, Joanna becomes a pawn in a much more sinister scheme—as past secrets, a priceless painting and a desperate killer create a masterpiece of murder.

"Joanna Stark, female sleuth, is brazen, courageous, feminine, but most of all convincing."

—*Mystery News*

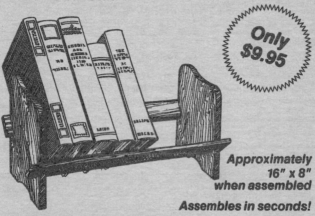

Order now the spine-tingling mysteries you missed in stores.

Don't miss these Worldwide Mysteries from award-winning authors!

MURDER MOST STRANGE—Dell Shannon $3.50 [ ]
Spring fever has hit Lieutenant Luis Mendoza both on the job and at
home. But it hasn't eased the LAPD's endless caseload of bizarre
crimes and difficult cases "Dapper Dan" the rapist and murderer ... a
stick-up artist who has found a foolproof weapon ... a gruesome
double homicide/suicide with a weird twist ... all add up to months of
Murder Most Strange, and Mendoza knows it's time to finally clean
house.

A QUESTION OF MURDER—Eric Wright $3.50 [ ]
Police inspector Charlie Salter is assigned to safeguard Toronto's
fashionable Yorkville section while the British princess is visiting. He
tries to control what looks like a feud between the business owners
and the street merchants when a bomb goes off, killing one of the
shopkeepers.

BOOKED FOR DEATH—Miriam Borgenicht $3.50 [ ]
Shortly after Celia Sommerville told her fiancé, George, that she
wouldn't marry him, his body turned up in a sleepy Vermont town.
Dead of a broken heart—and a self-inflicted gunshot wound. Celia is
determined to prove that cautious, pedantic George would not take his
own life. Her investigation reveals that a lot of people have reason to
want him dead. But who pulled the trigger?

Total Amount	$ _____
Plus 75¢ Postage	.75
Payment Enclosed	$ _____

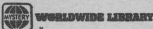